Book One

Surrendering Stinkin' Thinkin'

for Girls 10-100

You're

Beautiful

Hannah Arduini & Julie Arduini

Book 1,
Surrendering Stinkin' Thinkin' Series

You're Beautiful

Hannah Arduini

Julie Arduini

Surrendering Stinkin' Thinkin'

You're Beautiful---Hayley Atkinson withdraws from her friends and new opportunities with the new mentoring group, Linked, after she is told a lie that she believes is true about herself. Sabrina Wayson is a mentor in Linked who feels she can't encourage girls because she's struggling as much as they are. Can they surrender the lies and find freedom?

Coming Soon:

You're Amazing---Jazmin has always been a natural with dance, and now that she's in junior high, she's been promoted to an advanced group with older girls. For the first time, her favorite activity isn't easy, and she feels left out. Lena enjoyed going out with friends, but after getting married and having young children, she doesn't get invited out much anymore, and she finds motherhood exhausting. Can these two members of Linked let go of their frustration and realize how cherished they are?

You're Brilliant---Bethany has a lot of changes in her life as a new teenager, but she decides to tackle it with her offbeat humor. No one laughs with her, and even worse, her classmates abandon her, making Bethany feel rejected. Mrs. Cheri is a pastor's wife who loves her life, but new commitments have her overwhelmed. A joke aimed at her goes straight to her heart, and she's convinced she's not good at anything she's been asked to do. Can these two stop believing lies about themselves and embrace the changes in their life with laughter and grace?

A Message for Readers:

This series was inspired by Hannah after a tough transition to junior high. Instead of giving up and becoming bitter, Hannah decided to take the lessons she learned and create a series for girls her age. Julie (Hannah's mom,) has a passion for mentoring. As she listened to Hannah create characters, Julie realized there was a message in Hannah's work for women, too.

Each book in the Surrendering Stinkin' Thinkin' Series uses the theme of letting go of a lie the characters believed. There will be two key characters in each book. One, a junior high student, and the other, a woman out of school. It's our desire to see girls of all ages (even grandmas!) to read these books and find freedom and hope in them.

Hannah created the storyline, character names and traits, plot points, and conflict. She had the vision for the cover, and directed Julie in the design. Julie wrote out Hannah's vision and managed the writing and publishing process, staying true to Hannah's creation. *You're Beautiful* is a work of fiction, but a message of hope for you.

DEDICATION

To girls of all ages who have been told
or who have ever felt they were ugly.!

You are beautiful!

CHAPTER ONE
Hayley Atkinson

My palm print lands on the glass church doors as I push through and enter the lobby. This is my church, the one I've been to since birth, but my stomach isn't thrilled. Although my mom dropped me off for the new "Linked" mentoring ministry, my rolling nerves think we're still on the raft ride at the waterpark.

Before I can turn and head back to mom's car, Jazmin West taps me on the shoulder and giggles. "Hayley! You ready for this? It's going to be fun."

With Jazmin around, everything is fun. She's always smiling and dancing around.

"You think? Us girls and women sitting at a table talking? That doesn't sound exciting to me."

Jazmin rolls her eyes and takes me by the arm. "Who cares? They're having pizza. That's always fun for me."

Thing about Jazmin is she dances and moves all the time. Her metabolism is crazy high. She could eat ten pizzas and lose weight. Me? Not so much.

We find the Linked room upstairs in the youth department, a classroom with moveable walls and frayed artwork from kids who are probably in college now. Our pastor's wife, Mrs. Cheri, is already inside pouring something into plastic cups.

Jazmin skips over to her with a spontaneous hug. "Hey, Mrs. Cheri."

Our leader almost knocks over the filled cups, but looks at my friend, smiles, and tightens the hug. "Welcome, girls! I'm so glad you could be here. I don't know how many we'll have to start off tonight, but the saying is, 'Don't despise small beginnings.' Right?"

I put my phone on the table. "I guess."

Mrs. Cheri opens her arms and gestures me over. "C'mon, Hayley. I know you aren't a hugger, but it's happening."

She's right, I hate hugs. Yet with her, it's okay. Something about her makes her hugs feel like you've had a big chocolate chip cookie with M&M's without feeling guilty. "Do you know who is coming today?"

Mrs. Cheri resumes pouring punch into a cup. "The only others that called was the Green family."

My back stiffens as soon as I hear the name. Jade Green. My classmate since preschool. My peer in all church functions. And the entire time, my frenemy. She could greet me with a hug as nice as Mrs. Cheri's, or, walk past me and not even speak. I never know.

Jazmin glances at me, then Mrs. Cheri. "How about the leaders?"

She picks up a cup and takes a sip. "I didn't get as many answers as I had hoped. My niece, Sabrina, will be here. I think Lena Calloway will be here, too."

When I look over to Jazmin, she shrugs. We don't know that name.

Before we can ask about her, a stomping noise comes from the stairway area, and then footsteps come toward us. Bethany Tuttle bursts in with her messy bun of hair and jazz hands to greet us.

"Let the party start! I'm here!"

Mrs. Cheri opens those arms of hers and Bethany basically falls into them. "Bethy, I'm so glad you can be here. You're going to love Linked." She turns to us. "Why don't we all sit. We can chat while we wait."

Jazmin pulls out a chair. "Did you call her 'Bethy?'"

The two giggle. "I babysat Bethany for a couple months when Sabrina first moved in with us. Sabrina was six, I think. She was convinced that was Bethany's name. It stuck. At least with us Waysons'."

Bethany puts her fist under her chin and bats her eyes. "What can I say?"

Jazmin rolls her brown eyes. "Oh, brother."

Fifteen minutes later, Sabrina Wayson arrives, as well as Jade Green and Lena Calloway. Sabrina's fresh off her shift from the coffee shop, so she smells like vanilla and caramel. Lena is older than Sabrina, married, and has two little ones. Jade didn't say much when she walked through, just sat by Bethany and started texting. And I sit by Jazmin and Sabrina, my heart beating out of my chest.

Mrs. Cheri claps her hands together. "Ladies, I'm so happy to introduce you to our new generational ministry linking girls and ladies together. I'm Cheri Wayson, my husband is Pastor Chet. Encouraging others is a passion for me, and when Sabrina moved in with us, I saw how important it is for girls to be loved on. Build each other up with kind words and deeds." She looks to Lena. "And the more time I spend in ministry, the more I realize girls of all ages need reassurance. Here we are, with Linked."

Sabrina reaches for the drinks and starts passing the cups out until we each have one. "Mom and I have talked a lot about how Linked will work."

Jade lowers her phone and narrows her mint green eyes. "I thought Mrs. Cheri was your aunt."

I close my eyes so I don't roll them. Jazmin and Bethany know Sabrina's story just like anyone else at church who pays attention.

Sabrina smiles. "She is, but she also raised me. I consider her and Pastor Chet my parents, so I call them Mom and Dad."

Mrs. Cheri takes a sip of her drink. "I might not have given birth to her, but Sabrina is a daughter to us. She has great ideas, let's listen to her before the pizza arrives."

Jade raises the phone to eye level and continues to push buttons. Probably texting.

Sabrina pushes a blonde curl off her shoulder. "We're going to meet once a month here. Watch a video sometimes. Other meetings, read a devotional. Talk about it, but more than anything, just chat. Eat. Work on crafts. We also will do fun things outside of church. Maybe go out for frappes. Have a sleepover. Bowling night. Girl stuff."

Jazmin nudges my arm. I glance over and she's nodding. Looks like she's in.

I raise my hand. "Do we have to pay?"

Mrs. Cheri and Sabrina exchange looks. "Very rarely will something have a cost, and if so, we will keep the price low. If that's ever an issue for anyone, let me know. We will find a way. We'd rather have everyone join us than lose people because of money."

A knock followed by, "Pizza!" interrupts. Once Mrs. Cheri takes care of the bill and brings the hot boxes in, we leave our seats and gather around the food.

Lena giggles as she observes Jazmin dropping three pieces on her plate. "I thought my four-year-old ate a lot."

Jazmin tops her plate off with potato chips. "One thing about Linked. You better bring a lot of food."

Mrs. Cheri pushes her plate aside after prayer while the rest of us stuff our faces. "I thought I'd use the rest of the time to get to know each other. Is it okay if we ask each other questions? You can pass if you want, and you can ask Sabrina, Lena and me, too."

Bethany wipes her chin with a napkin. "Works for me."

The rest of us nod.

Sabrina glances around the table and rests her gaze on me. "Hayley. What would you like to do if money was no object?"

I instantly picture blue waters and the ship we went on when I was nine. "Disney cruise."

Jazmin still has a little pizza left to chew, but asks, "Why?"

I shrug. "It was fun. There was something for everyone to do. The food was amazing."

Jade snorts, but keeps eating.

Bethany either ignores her or doesn't hear her, and focuses on me. "I'd love to go on one of those, too."

Our questions range from favorite subject in school to crushes on boys to favorite movies. When it's time to dismiss, Mrs.

Cheri stands with her arms extended. "Girls, this has been such a treat. We'll be in touch with your parents to receive permission to text or message you updates or to send along a prayer or encouragement." She hugs Bethany, then Jade.

Sabrina stands next to me and touches my arm. "If you like frappes, we should have a girls' night at Mugs. What do you think?"

Mugs is the coffee shop and bakery for teens. No one makes a better hot chocolate or cookie dough iced coffee. "I'd love it."

As we walk to youth group, we give our thoughts on the new ministry.

Jazmin rubs her stomach. "That was the best pizza. I think this is going to be awesome."

Bethany nods. "They seem nice. Lena is shy, but I think we'll have fun."

Bass sounds bounce off the walls as we enter the youth area. "I love that Sabrina goes to Mugs. Won't it be fun to meet there?"

Jazmin and Bethany agree, while Jade shoots me a scowl.

I breathe deep. "Jade, don't you like iced coffees?"

She rolls her eyes, which sends my anger even higher because I was tempted to do the same with her and didn't. "I love it. I just don't want to go with you."

CHAPTER TWO
Sabrina Wayson

Shannon Price and I attempt to walk up to the mall kiosk as if getting our noses pierced is no big deal. Once I reach the glass countertop, I rest my elbow on it, nearly knocking over the display that drew us there to begin with: *"Buy One Piercing, Get the Second Half Off."*

The clerk, who looks about my age, snaps her gum as she puts her phone down. "Can I help you?"

Shannon steps forward to the counter. My BFF since I moved to Youngstown is usually the ringleader in our hijinks. "Two nose piercings." Her voice falters toward the end. "I mean, one nose piercing, but for each of us." Her shaky hand points to her nose first, then mine.

The girl snaps the minty gum again. "Who goes first?"

Shannon shrugs and takes a tiny step back.

I sigh and raise my hand. As the young woman gestures for me to go to the side where she swings the counter up, I turn back to my friend. "Chicken."

Twenty minutes later I'm fighting back a few tears, the sudden urge to sneeze, and a badge of pride in the shape of a sparkly stud through my nose.

Shannon's strut isn't nearly as confident. "She said it would sting. I feel like I got shot."

My stride moves in the direction of the food court. "Well, it is called a piercing gun."

Before she can respond, she pulls me back by the arm and swings me against the wall. "I think your dad's here."

I squint and remove myself from the wall. "I told you he's okay with it. I'm twenty-one."

Her hand takes a lump of my arm flesh and twists it, keeping me frozen in place and no longer focusing on the ring pain. "Sabrina, your biological dad."

Now I feel like I've been shot, in the heart. I peer ahead and see a taller, tatted likeness ordering pizza. "Ugh. I'm not up for this."

Shannon releases her death grip. "We can leave."

I wave her off. "No. This was our plan and no one's going to stop us. C'mon, we have mediocre mall food to indulge in."

We march in sync to the food court, and I want pizza. Ever since the Linked meeting, my body craves it. If I want to satisfy that need, I've got to get in line. And see my dad.

"I was going to get Chinese. Do you care, Sabrina?"

I breathe in slowly, and exhale just as slow. "No. Go ahead. I'll be okay."

Shannon stares into my eyes. "You sure?"

"Yeah. He can't hurt me worse than the piercing, right?"

She smiles and leaves me for Orient Express. I take out my phone and decide the "head down, engrossed in phone" position is best. As I move to the front, Dad's to the left, waiting for his tray.

Rod Wayson waves to get my attention, which is ironic given my pre-school years were all about me doing something, anything, for my parents to choose to spend time with me over their addictions. "Sabrina?"

I shove my phone in my pocket and feign surprise, pushing guilt into deeper pockets only Jesus could empty. "Hey."

He steps forward and joins me. "Long time no see. Still living with my preacher brother?"

If you'd call, text or visit any of us, you'd know.

"I'm with my parents, yes. How about you?"

He rubs his greying goatee. "I have a job and place in Austintown. Not far from Chet's church, actually. I'm cleaning up my act." He's said that so many times it could be a song.

I give my order and move to the side, silently praying his pizza is waiting for him. He makes no move to the pick-up line, and that only accelerates my dread.

Rod's eyes widen. "Is that a nose ring? There's no way Cheri allowed that."

"She did. I am an adult, after all." My tone is flat and I push down the snark that only one of us in the conversation is.

He grins, almost as if I achieved greatness in his eyes. Forget my education degree, my steady job and place on the worship team. It's the nose ring that has his approval. "Looks good on you. Maybe now the boys will start paying attention to you, right?"

My back stiffens, shocked by the blow that usually comes when he's under the influence. "Dating really hasn't been a priority."

He nods. "Of course. But being done with school, it's about time, right? Need to land yourself a husband."

Seriously. I don't live in the 1870's prairie.

"I'm sure God will provide, like everything else." Like healthy parents.

A teenaged voice calls his name and Dad looks to his tray. "It's a shame, though. I just don't want you alone like me. You have a cute face, but men want the whole package. Not just a brain."

With every word, a thousand knives carve up my confidence. I can't move, or speak.

"Your mom didn't add the pounds until after the divorce and her boyfriend left her. Serves her right, cheating on me. Anyway, you need to be careful. Women, even your friends, will do anything to get in the game and get a man. Make sure you have competitive edge." He scans me up and down. "The nose ring helps. Well, gotta eat my dinner before meeting the guys for poker. Good seeing you."

He has no idea I didn't say goodbye or even move. When my name's called, the tray sits there, neglected and alone. Something I can totally relate to.

CHAPTER THREE
HAYLEY

It's been a couple weeks since the Linked meeting and Jade's snide comment. I'm over it, okay, nearly over it, avoiding her as I usually do after she's been rude. Mom wants to take me school shopping, not my favorite, but she's offered to let me try on the new Adidas for possible purchase. That battle's two years in the making, so I'm ready to spend the day with her.

We fight through the crowds for the boring supplies before Mom announces it's time to drive to the mall for clothes and shoes. I spot Mugs on the way and point in the direction.

Although she's driving, she sees what I'm up to and nods. "I could use the caffeine."

Mom winces as soon as she opens the door. The familiar refrain of my favorite boy band song I've played all summer hits as soon as we enter.

I march ahead, ready for that cookie dough iced coffee. Mom trails behind, but not too far. When I gesture for her to join me in line, I notice Jade in a booth with high school girls.

Their laughter draws attention, even Mom's. "Isn't that Jade? Are you going to say hello?"

She has no idea that the hot-cold status between Jade and I never stopped in elementary school.

I swat the idea away like a fly at a picnic. "No, she looks busy."

Mom mumbles as she hands her card to the cashier. "You'll see her soon enough with the Linked meeting coming up, right?"

"Sure."

We complete the transaction and take our drinks to go. I don't look toward Jade and her friends, so I have no idea if their laughter is aimed at me. Some things are better left unknown.

Somehow, I manage to stay away from Jade until the day before Linked. Mom has me in this summer Y program for exercise, and of course, Jade's in it, too. This week's my least favorite activity, kickball, when the coach places us on the same team. I'm in line praying someone budges ahead when Jade sidles up to me.

"Saw you at Mugs. With your mom."

I purse my lips and nod.

"Did you see me? I was with the freshmen."

Let's keep this as silent as possible. I shrug.

She's non-deterred. "Trina says that only plebes go to Mugs with their mommies."

I can't help it, I roll my eyes. The very definition of plebe means freshman, of which Trina is one. But I know Jade's going for the mean-girl definition.

Jade sighs. "I'm surprised you even went inside. There's no way that place is for you."

I cross my arms, still praying my turn at the plate never happens. "Jade, what are you yammering on about?"

"Mugs is for popular people. I go there, Trina. Cassie. Even Bethany and Jazmin belong there. But you?" Her eyes narrow and she pinches up her nose as if she'd just touched a dead fish. "You'll never belong."

"Why? Except for Trina and Cassie, we're all in the same grade."

Jade offers a sickly-sweet smile. "Oh, I know. It's more than that. Everyone else belongs because they are pretty. And I don't mean pretty ugly."

I'm so stunned by her direct hit that I don't see the kickball coming my way. To prove Jade's point, the red ball comes at me as fast as a missile, and I leave gym class for the nurse's office with a black eye and bruised heart.

Jazmin's the first to find me after school. I'm tempted to hide my entire face in the locker because my mirror shows a purple shiner only getting uglier on my right eye. My friend grabs me by the shoulder and turns me toward her.

"It's true! Did Jade really hit you?"

I reach for a folder and cover my eye. "No. A ball came at me at the same time as Jade's commentary."

Jazmin lowers the binder. "It's as purple as that dinosaur we watched when we were kids."

Angry tears sting my good eye. "Can we talk about something else?"

She nods. "Do you need a ride to Linked? Mom said she can take you."

Jade's words puncture my mind all over again. I don't belong. I'm not just ugly, but pretty ugly. The thoughts travel from my head to my heart, and reside there with such speed I feel dizzy. "I'll get back to you. I'm not sure what the plans are yet."

She raises an eyebrow but doesn't respond.

At least one prayer has been answered.

CHAPTER FOUR
SABRINA

The August sun does nothing to motivate me on my day off. Dad's words hang over me like a black cloud. Chalking up his conversation to ignorance and addiction doesn't work because he's right. My dating history is nearly a blank page. Most guys see me as their buddy. And I want to snack and sleep my way through my feelings.

"Sabrina? Are you busy?" Mom's cheery voice breaks through my darkening thoughts. Her blonde curls bounce as the walks in my room.

I look down at my faded youth-camp shirt and pajama shorts. "Not really. What's up?"

She sighs. "My schedule got away from me, and I need to prepare for the Linked meeting. Would you text the girls and remind them to come? Give them some encouragement?"

I glance at my phone, hoping the battery's low. It's almost a full charge. "What kind of encouragement?"

"Let them know we love them and have been praying for them. That they are treasured and highly valuable in their Heavenly Father's eyes. You're a natural with positive words. I also wondered about a topic." Mom holds up a pair of leggings. "Do we talk about modesty, or, beauty?"

I close my eyes for a moment. There's no way I want to tackle how attractive we all are when my father lectured me on watching my weight so I can land a man. "I've seen enough crop tops and yoga pants to say modesty is a good subject to start with."

Mom bites her lip. "True. But low self-esteem is such a problem. If we don't tackle that, the girls will probably let their insecurities on beauty come out in their clothes and make-up choices."

She has a point. "I'll keep praying about it. Would you want to share a testimony or your observations on either idea?"

My throat feels as if I ate sand for breakfast. "Oh, no. You'll be great, Mom."

She shakes her head. "Sweetheart, the girls will respond better to you because you're closer to their age. Pray about it, would you? I need to run to the store and get a veggie tray and dip."

Before I can reply, she rubs my arm as she exits, leaving me with my phone and a challenge I'm completely ill-equipped to complete.

After two cups of coffee, I dress and create the reminder texts. I start with Jazmin, filling my message with pizza and heart emojis.

She immediately replies with a thumb's up. *Can't wait! See you tomorrow!*

Bethany answers a few minutes later. Her text shows twice as many visuals, some I don't even know what they are. *It's gonna be lit, Sabrina!*

Jade shares a simple, *Thx*, and I don't know if I should try to keep the chat going. I still have Hayley to contact, so I let it go, thumbs moving across the screen as I contact Hayley.

While I wait to hear from her, I open Facebook and scroll my newsfeed. Five minutes become ten, and after an hour, I realize Hayley hasn't written back. I text again.

Hey, girl! Making sure you got my message. See you tomorrow at Linked. Remember you are amazing and God loves you so much!

As I type, my throat constricts, a growing part of me wishing someone would text this affirmation to me. With a deep breath, I focus on Hayley and forget my problems. She doesn't respond, so I text Lena, the other mentor.

She answers with mom wisdom I wouldn't have thought of. Maybe she's grounded and lost her phone. Maybe she's traveling and doesn't have signal.

I nod, forgetting I'm alone and no one's interacting with me. But something in the pit of my stomach stays with me long after I stop texting. Hayley needs prayer. And although I don't think anything I say is going to be a huge help to anyone, the feeling is something I can't ignore.

"Father God, I ask that You be with Hayley, whatever is going on with her, give her courage. Help her feel Your love for her, and our love, too. Bless us with words of encouragement for her. Thank You for taking care of her. Amen."

My room remains silent as I close the laptop and pick up my phone. Hayley still hasn't replied. I close my eyes and lay back on my bed, the headboard's creak bouncing off the walls. Once everything is quiet, the thoughts return with the force of a hurricane.

I'm not enough.

I'm just a buddy.

I can't land a man.

I'm not pretty.

I'm overweight.

I'm nothing.

By the time I sit back up, I'm dizzy with dread. There's no way I can go to Linked feeling like this. I've got to get out of that meeting before the girls find out what a fraud I am.

CHAPTER FIVE
HAYLEY

It isn't right, but in order to skip Linked, I have to play sick. Mom's rule is no school, no night activities. However, school hasn't started yet. So, courtesy of a hot thermometer, a heating pad, and some drama, my parents believe I'm sick.

Mom leaves me directions for soup and suggests I drink hot tea. I don't want either one in August. Instead, I hop on the couch with my phone and turn on the TV. I binge watch a new show on Netflix and take a little nap until the doorbell rings.

I groan and sit up. "Who is it?"

Bethany's annoyed voice comes through. "Open up."

"Just a sec."

When I unlock and swing the door wide for her to walk past, Bethany meets me with a hard stare. "Sick people don't answer the door."

I furrow my brow, not sure how she knows what's going on. "Who told you I was sick?"

Bethany strides past me and plops on the couch. "Your mom texted mine and asked her to look out for you. Kind of a coincidence you're sick the day of Linked."

I attempt to give a confident response by staring right back. "I needed a day to myself."

"Uh-huh. Is this about Jade? Jazmin told me she's been bothering you again." Bethany hugs my pillow. "Why won't you say something? I could help. Or your parents. Even Mrs. Cheri."

I join her on the couch, reaching for another pillow. "You're giving Jade way too much credit. I wanted a day to myself, that's it."

She sits cross-legged. "So, you'll be at Linked."

It's hard not to smile. "No, house rule. If you miss school you can't go anywhere at night. It's the same for summer stuff. If I can't make it through the day, then no evening activities."

Bethany rolls her eyes. "How convenient, Hayley. Why won't you let us help? I'm your friend."

Jade's words come back on me like mom's leftovers, no matter how I try to push them out of my thoughts.

Pretty.

I'm not pretty.

In fact, I'm pretty ugly.

It's not easy to force my voice to sound normal when tears are ready to fall. "I'm fine. Really. I'll be at the pool to hang out tomorrow."

She shoots me a look with a raised eyebrow. "You're sure you're okay?"

I fake a smile. "Yep."

"Maybe we can go to Mugs after swimming."

My smile disappears. *Only the best go there. It's not a place for me.* "We'll see."

She stands. "Awesome. See you tomorrow."

I walk her to the door and wave before she walks away. Then I shut the door, and slump against it while I exhale a few hot breaths. When I finally move, I nose-dive onto the couch, punching pillows until there's no fight left.

CHAPTER SIX
SABRINA

My idea bank overdrafts as I try to think of an excuse that will get me out of going to Linked. I need to go to work, so I can't play sick. Cramps are an easy excuse, but Mom will pray, give me ibuprofen, and tell me to get in the car. Telling her I don't feel up to it isn't going to get me anywhere, either. She'll take my insecurities and use them as the reason I need to go. So the girls know we struggle, too. But the truth is Mom and Lena are better role models for the girls.

Mom interrupts my thinking as I saunter into the kitchen for breakfast. "Sabrina, are you coming here before Linked? I need help with the veggie tray and dip."

I shrug. "I'm not sure. I might have to work late. I forgot, I think tonight is inventory night." My hands moisten.

She sighs. "Sabrina, didn't you tell them you had plans? This is important. The girls are counting on you."

I walk to the fridge and take out the juice. "Inventories are mandatory. It slipped my mind that it was the same night as Linked."

She pulls her keys out of her purse. "Okay, I'll run upstairs and ask Chet if he can take the tray and dip to work and put it in the church fridge."

Sounds like a plan.

Once Mom jogs downstairs, her sweet voice stabs at my conscience. "I'm off to work. Seems like I won't see you tonight. Praying you have a great day." She starts for the front door. "And inventory."

Not only am I not worthy to land a man, but now I'm also a liar.

The guilt from lying grows on me like ivy on a church. By the end of my shift, I'm sick with regret. After everything my parents have done to raise me, I can't let Mom down. I decide to attend the meeting, and stop at Mugs for a tray of frappes to surprise the girls at church.

Before I cross the threshold to the room, Jazmin and Jade leap from their chairs and run over. Jazmin reaches for a chocolate drink and takes a sip, leaving a whipped-cream mustache.

Bethany shakes her head as she patiently waits at her seat. "Sabrina didn't say that was for us."

Jade raises her cup. "Why else would she be carrying them?" She turns toward me. "Thanks, Sabrina."

I place the carrier on the table. "No problem."

Mom turns and smiles. "What happened with inventory?"

I mentally brace myself for impact as I prepare for another lie. "I got the date wrong."

She pats me on the shoulder. "It's an answer to prayer. Thanks for the drinks, Chet forgot the veggie tray at home, so this is our snack."

Lena sips her drink. "I'm definitely not complaining, and I don't think the girls are, either."

Once we settle, Mom opens with prayer and announces she's going to talk about modesty for a few minutes. I scan the room and realize someone's missing. Hayley.

I speak up as Mom reaches for a bag and pulls out leggings. "Girls, where's Hayley?"

Jazmin shrugs. Jade's looking down past the table, my guess is she's trying to hide her texting. Bethany pays a lot of attention to her drink.

I lean in toward the table. "Bethy? Know anything about her?"

She bites her lip. "She wasn't feeling well." When she puts her cup down, she shoots a look toward Jade.

I glance to Mom, but she's getting outfits ready to display. Lena stifles a yawn and takes a sip of her frappe.

My focus is on Bethy. "Oh. That's too bad. We should check up on her."

Jazmin and Bethany nod while I take my phone out and create a reminder. Despite my failings in so many departments, there's something about Hayley that makes me think she's in trouble. And that I'm meant to help her., somehow.

Mom claps her hands and displays a wide smile. "Let's chat. I put together some outfits, and I thought we could talk about what works or doesn't work when it comes to dressing appropriately."

The girls stand and walk over, examining the clothes. Jade's drawn to a short miniskirt, crop top and jean jacket. Bethany nudges Jazmin and they point at a pair of leggings complemented with a dress and a long sweater.

Jade holds up the denim jacket. "My sister has one like this. She never lets me borrow it."

Mom joins her. "What about the outfit? Is this something that promotes modesty?"

She shrugs. "No clue. I just think it's adorbs."

Mom tries again. "It is cute, but you know what would make it even better?"

Jade mumbles, still admiring the coat.

"Leggings. You don't want to show too much skin, and this skirt is quite short. Leggings fix that."

Bethany nods. "Sabrina, you've worn outfits like that with leggings."

"Yes. I can bend over without being embarrassed, and I don't make it difficult for boys. They don't need to see my flesh."

A sarcastic laugh comes from Jade. "Maybe you don't."

Mom's eyes widen. "What do you mean, honey?"

Jazmin and Bethany don't even appear to blink as they put their elbows on the table and shift their chairs closer.

Another shrug from Jade. "Popular girls want to be noticed. Only Plebes would cover up like that. It's not that short."

Lena sits up. "What's a Plebe?"

Jazmin jumps in the fray. "The high school girls label everyone, and that's who Jade hangs out with. Plebes should be the freshmen, but it is really a term for anyone not cool or popular."

Jade doesn't seem put off by the explanation at all. "I'm already invited to sit with older girls at Mugs. They say to catch an amazing boyfriend, you need to let them know you exist. Put yourself out there. And this outfit is a way to do that."

I gulp, hearing the same phrase my dad used for me. Put myself out there. I don't know where the lead anchor in my stomach is from----his words flooding back---or Jade's logic.

CHAPTER SEVEN
HAYLEY

The iron gate at the entrance to the community pool squeaks as I push it open. The sunbathers and lifeguards swing their heads toward me, and every time my wide feet hit the hot pavement with what I believe mimics an elephant on the loose, I'm tempted to turn around and sneak back to my house. Bethany jumps up from her lounge chair and waves, leaving me little choice but to join her.

She lifts her towel off the chaise next to her. "Glad you're feeling better."

I plop down on the seat. "You can stop with the guilt trip now. Sabrina and Mrs. Cheri texted me, saying they missed me. I wasn't up for it."

Bethany pulls out her bottle of sunscreen and pours some into the palm of her hand. "It's a shame. Sabrina brought frappes. Mrs. Cheri gave a presentation on modesty and Jade jacked it up. It was kind of crazy."

"What happened?"

She hands the bottle over. "Jade liked all the outfits the mentors were telling us not to wear. She declared that popular girls wear short skirts for attention, and that it's okay. I thought Mrs. Cheri was going to faint."

I shake my head. "Wow. Did Jade behave other than that?"

Bethy shrugs. "Why do you care? You said she wasn't a problem."

Too much sunscreen squirts out, and I attempt to spread it all over my neck, arms and legs. "I'm just curious."

"Whatever. You know we've got your back. So does Mrs. Cheri, Lena, and Sabrina. If Jade threatened you, we can help."

Joey Leonard, a thrill seeker from my homeroom, jumps in the water cannonball style, sending a wave of water right at Bethany and me.

Marcy Butler, a freshman who wears the tight skirts Jade loves so much, walks by, getting drenched as she passes us. She shakes her arms and head, sending more droplets our way. "Ugh. You Plebe! Could you learn how to dive like an adult?"

Her anger only makes Joey laugh. She narrows her gaze and snarls at us. "What are you two looking at? Shouldn't you be at the kiddie pool?"

Marcy's outburst brings a tidal wave of emotions. Jade's sneer comes to mind, with all the things she's said. *I don't belong. I'm nothing. I'm ugly. I'm not invited to the popular places.*

Bethany doesn't seem bothered. "What? Are you afraid your paper-thin bikini will disintegrate because Joey splashed you?"

Marcy rolls her eyes and stalks off. Joe's laughter, along with all Jade's insults, assaults my thoughts. I drop the sunscreen, spilling some on the cement.

"Hayley, be careful. Mom said this stuff is expensive."

I try to slide some of the white goo back into the bottle. "Sorry, I think I'll go home. It's hotter than I thought out here, and the sun's giving me a headache."

Bethany cocks her head. "You just got here. What's going on?"

More boys jump in, water erupting toward us as I gather my things. "I don't feel well."

She stands, wiping her arms with her towel. "Is it Marcy? She's cranky because her hair got messed up. It wasn't personal."

I stand, tote bag in hand. "I know. I have a headache, and the chaos here isn't helping."

Bethy looks at her phone. "I don't have to be home for another hour. How about we cure that headache with a trip to Mugs?"

The mention of the coffee shop sends dread to my toes. I shake my head. "No, I can't. Thanks, though."

She furrows her brow. "You're sure? You never turn down a frappe."

I know. But they go to my thighs.
Another fact that makes me pretty ugly.

38

As I wave goodbye and return to the gate, my focus is on the negative commentary running through my mind. With my head down, I scuff against the pavement, hating myself more with each step.

Nothing.

Less than nothing.

Unpopular.

My breathing hitches when I collide with something. I look up and see a woman holding an overstuffed beach bag. "I'm sorry, I wasn't paying attention."

The woman looks to her sides where two young children stand. She reaches out a hand to my shoulder. "Apparently not, Hayley. It's me, Lena, from Linked. Are you okay?"

I nod. "Ms. Lena. Right." I run a hand through my thick hair. "I'm fine. Headed home."

The boy grabs his mom's bag and pulls. "Let's go."

Ms. Lena pats his head. "One minute, please." She looks at me and smiles. "You're welcome to join us. I brought peanut butter and jelly sandwiches."

"Thanks, but I'm going to pass. Maybe another time."

She opens her arms for a quick hug. "I'll take you up on that. Hayley, you have my number. Don't be afraid to use it. For anything."

"I know. I will. Enjoy your swim."

The kids tear off toward the kiddie area while I push on the noisy gate. Kicking pebbles as I walk home, I stop in front of Mugs. My chest tightens as I picture Jade's sneer when she mocked me in gym class. As I peer through the window, a group of girls in a booth throw their heads back in laughter before retrieving phones to take selfies. One of the girls turns around and seems to look out toward me as I look in. Whether the girl with braces and a set of keys nearby notices me or not, part of me hopes she will smile. Say "hello." Wave, maybe.

The other part of me remembers rejection, so it's little surprise when she turns back to her squad and resumes the laughter, while I return to kicking stones. Alone.

CHAPTER EIGHT
SABRINA

Mid-August brings more traffic to the coffee shop as drinkers of all things pumpkin spice are hoping for the fall menu while the summer customers still order the iced beverages. All I know is the line doesn't seem to have an end when my shift starts.

My manager, Kane, slides next to me with a frappe cup. "Sabrina, I need the caramel."

Without looking at him, I move the bottle next to him and glance at the next customer in line. "Mrs. Tunney. Getting ready for school?"

The principal of the junior and high school smiles. "That's why I'm here. Administrators are already back to work, and I thought I'd bring some caffeine for them. Here's the list of what I need."

I take the paper and nod. Two mocha lattes, a chai tea, and three caramel frappes. Not too hard of an order to make.

"Remind me, Sabrina, did you graduate college? I get my alumni mixed up."

I take the caramel back from Kane. "Yes, in May. I have my Bachelor's now."

Mrs. Tunney bites her lip. "Help me remember. Education?"

"You don't give yourself enough credit. Secondary education."

"I found out yesterday that Mrs. Styles wants to extend her time off after the baby. She doesn't plan to return until the new year. Are you interested in interviewing to be her long-term sub?"

I almost drop the whipped cream can. "Absolutely."

She digs in her purse and pulls out a card. "If you get done here before five, call me, and we'll set something up."

My arms shake as I place the drinks in a carrier and hand it to her. "Thank you, I definitely will."

Once she leaves, I turn to the other barista, Vanessa, and let out a squeal.

Kane turns toward me and points to the ever-present line of customers. "Stay focused, Sabrina."

"Right. Sorry." Before I take the next order, I look at the clock. Two more hours before I can go home and make that call.

My last customer is Charlie Shell, a regular black coffee and my friend since I moved into the neighborhood. "Ready to switch it up and order something new?"

Charlie rakes his hand through his thick, jet-black hair and chuckles. "Never. I need the high-octane stuff to power through my grad schedule." He cranes his neck toward the bakery case. "Do you have any blueberry muffins? I'll have one to go, if you do." Charlie locks eyes with me as I hand him his drink. "What are you up to? Are you still riding your bike around the area? I haven't seen you."

I didn't think anyone noticed I haven't quite been exercising on a regular basis. "Working here a lot. I help my parents at church. There's a new ministry with teen girls that I'm involved with. And…" I sneak another glance at his cocoa-colored eyes and grin. "Mrs. Tunney told me about a long-term sub job. I plan to call her once my shift is done."

Charlie's crooked smile, something I've seen for years, somehow syncs to my accelerating heartbeat. He gives me his credit card, our hands graze during the exchange. "Sabrina, that's great. I'll be praying for you. Keep me posted, okay?"

I complete the transaction and nod. "Don't work too hard."

He opens the door and turns to me. "Right back at ya."

Vanessa nudges me as she walks by. "Someone's having a great day."

Mrs. Tunney answers my call after the third ring, and we make an appointment for Friday afternoon. If I could get my foot in the door with the school system, other districts would like my experience. I love serving coffee, but it isn't my career goal.

Dad's in the dining room, pulling a chair out for mom when I saunter down the stairs. I can spot his dimples, that same boyish grin mom said she fell in love with the first time they met. "You look extra happy today. What's new?"

He helps me into my seat, and the tantalizing aroma of roast beef dances around my nose. I lay my napkin down and smile wide. "I have an interview with Mrs. Tunney for a long-term sub job."

Mom lowers the serving fork. "Sabrina, that's fantastic! When is it?"

"Friday. Enough time to brush up on my public speaking skills."

Dad passes the bowl of mashed potatoes. "You're going to be excellent. I told Gloria Tunney that right after she told me about the vacancy."

The spoon drops into a heap of creamy fluff. "What did you say?"

He pierces a piece of roast beef and places it on his plate. "I saw Gloria yesterday at the store. Asked her how things were going at school, haven't heard much since the joint church and school board meeting. She told me about the vacancy and I mentioned you. Told her you worked at the coffee shop."

I almost drop the bowl. "You sent her to me? Now she's obligated to interview me because the church founded the school and you oversee the board. Nothing like being a pity case."

You're Beautiful

CHAPTER NINE
HAYLEY

Beth's brother pulls up in front of the mall food court entrance and shifts into park. "Mom said you need to be out here in two hours. Don't be late, I didn't get my license to drive you girls around."

Beth, Jazmin, and I roll our eyes and stifle a laugh. We gather our purses and slide out of the vehicle using the slam of the door as our goodbye.

Jazmin's the first to chuckle. "Your brother is cranky."

Beth opens the heavy glass door. "Aaron's mad. He thought when once he got his license, our parents would buy him a sports car, and he'd drive around Austintown with girls begging to date him."

Our giggles bounce off the food court walls and Jazmin shakes her head. "That's messed up."

I nod. "True, but two hours isn't a long time. School starts in two weeks, and mom gave me money for clothes. I need to find something awesome for the first day."

Jazmin sighs. "Tell me there's time for food. I need pizza."

Beth points ahead. "Oh, look, Forever 21. They have the new shirts I was talking about. Let's go."

The two take off faster than the best runner on the high school track team. I pick up my pace, but lag behind as I fight the uneasiness growing in my stomach. *I'm not sure I'll be able to find the perfect outfit, and I really want the first day to be a great one.*

Forty minutes later, we've picked over every t-shirt in Forever 21. Jazmin also bought a pretzel, we sprayed on sample perfumes at Macy's, and now they are in the jean section trying to find their size.

I put my hands on my hips. "We haven't even looked for my outfit yet. You know I don't wear jeans. Can we look at leggings now?"

Beth puts a pair of faded jeans back on the rack. "Sorry. Let's go to The Phoenix. I love their clothes, too."

I wince. "They don't have my..."

Jazmin puts the denim back and starts for the exit. "I love The Phoenix."

They march toward their destination before I can finish. "...size."

Twenty minutes left before Beth's brother picks us up and the girls throw three pair of jeans over the dressing room door.

I sigh as I pull my leggings down. "Didn't the sign say only three items at a time? I already have a pair of jeans and two shirts."

Jazmin expels her own hot air. "You don't have time to argue. It's fine. We'll put anything back you don't want."

I pick up the first pair of jeans and stretch them at the waist. *Please fit. Please let one pair fit.* I jam one leg in, the other, then pull up to place over my stomach. The button has no intention of uniting with the hole. With several yanks, I take the first pair off and throw them aside.

"You okay in there?" Beth whispers from the other side of the dressing room door.

"Is anyone ever okay trying on clothes?"

Jazmin chuckles. "She has a point. There are times my mom comes out with tears in her eyes and announces those things would have fit when she was single."

I hear the two chatter on about their moms as I try on the second pair. Same result. Another pair of too-tight jeans land in a pile. I repeat the pattern until I'm down to the last shirt and jeans.

Beth's revelation flows through the dressing room. "If you buy the striped shirt, we'd have a similar outfit."

I kick at the discarded pile. "I'm almost done." The gold button comes close to the hole, but not close enough. The striped shirt cuts off my arm circulation and clings to my belly.

Jazmin's voice is next. "I tried the striped one on, but I didn't like it. Too baggy."

If only.

With my own clothes on, I pick up the others and leave. "I need these on hangers."

The two exchange looks, but I can't tell what they're conveying.

"All of them go back?" Beth's voice isn't much more of a whisper.

I refuse to focus anywhere but on the hanger and jeans I'm fighting with. I nod, finish the task, and throw the pants on the rack before marching out in a sulk.

No one says anything as we leave the store and head to the food court exit. Beth catches up without a lot of effort and touches my shoulder. "You okay?"

"The clothes didn't fit."

Jazmin flanks my other side. "That store can be weird with sizes."

I stop and squeeze my eyes shut for a moment as I try to process my emotions. When I open them, the two stand next to each other, facing me with blank stares. "You don't get it. I can't shop where you two do. It isn't that easy for me. I don't fit in any of the clothes in any of those stores. It isn't the sizing. It's me."

Bethany closes the gap between us. "I didn't know. I'm so sorry. It was really insensitive of me."

Jazmin lowers her head. "Rude of both of us. How can we help?"

I look past the door and see Beth's brother's car at the curb. "Just take me home."

You're Beautiful

48

CHAPTER TEN
SABRINA

I smooth the wrinkles out of my blazer and take a deep breath. The mirror pulls no punches, and I wish I'd resisted the ice cream after dinner last night. And any I'd enjoyed all summer.

"Sabrina, you look so professional." Mom walks into the hallway and smiles.

"Let's hope Mrs. Tunney agrees."

"You do know just because your dad pastors the church that founded the school, it means nothing when it comes to staffing, right?"

I shrug. "I'm sure he meant well when he told her to find me at the shop and talk about the job opening."

She nods. "He never intended it to look like he was manipulating her interview you out of pity."

"It does feel that way. You get that, right?"

Mom rests her hand on my arm. "Sabrina. I understand you experienced manipulation and obligation with your birth parents. Even if your father is my brother-in-law, you need to remember we don't operate that way. We never have. Now, how about I pray and you crush that interview."

I chuckle as I allow a hug. "You sound like the girls from Linked."

She winks. "If you get the job, you'll be working with them, and girls who talk like that all the time."

The school hallways seem smaller than I remember, but the smells and lockers in need of new paint remain the same as the day I received my diploma. I wait in the hallway by the office in a plastic chair, tapping my foot to the newest Mandisa song playing on the office radio.

Not long after the song ends, Mrs. Tunney pokes her head out of the doorway. "Sabrina, I'm sorry I kept you waiting. I had to resolve a class list issue. Come on in."

I inhale slowly and take my time breathing out as I sit in the chair opposite her desk. "Thank you for interviewing me today."

She takes a seat and shuffles through folders on her desk, pulling one up. "I'm glad Pastor Chet said something when I saw him the other day. I apologize for not keeping track of your college graduation date. You were an excellent student here, and I remember you wanted to study education."

I nod, willing my heartbeat to steady. "Yes. I graduated in May from Kent State, and am signed up for a couple online grad classes in the fall."

"Did you bring your resume and transcript?"

I produce my own folder, and hand it to her. "What those don't say is that I recently joined a new mentoring ministry that connects women of all ages to teen girls for mentoring purposes."

She peruses the paperwork. "What has been the biggest challenge working with that age group?"

Ideas roll as fast as a game show wheel before I reply. "It's important to me that I connect with each girl, even if we don't have a lot in common. Some girls relate to me better than others, but I don't want to forget or ignore anyone."

Her smile calms my nerves. "The students who need the most encouragement are often the quiet ones, or even the obnoxious ones. They need more time, and we have to work hard to earn their trust."

Hayley and Jade come to mind.

"What kind of a problem solver are you?"

The kind that brings frappes? "I like to use words, affirming ones, of course. I believe a lot more can be accomplished with building people up."

Mrs. Tunney makes a couple notes on one of the papers in front of her. "How involved would you be with conflict resolution between students?"

Something tells me this is a big question with a lot hinging on my response. "The kids involved would probably think I was staying out of it, but the reality is I would be watching closely, and I would be praying. My ultimate goal would be for the participating parties to resolve things themselves. However, if it got physical or I witnessed any kind of bullying, I would step in."

More scribbling. "Middle school students have additional challenges of struggling with self-worth and confidence, and that often can be tied to their academic performance. What's your strategy to combat this?"

"That's a great question, because I remember not feeling very good about myself in junior high." Or now. "I think it goes back to words. The Bible is my guide, and it says 'the power of life and death are in the tongue.' My hope as a teacher at any level is to be one that builds kids up, not tear them down."

My grip on the armrest is so strong that my wrist aches. The questions continue along the line of following lesson plans and discipline.

Twenty minutes later, Mrs. Tunney pushes her papers back and stands. "Sabrina, I appreciate your time. There are a few more candidates to interview, but I hope to make a decision by the end of the week. I will be calling everyone with my decision."

We shake hands and I thank her once again, barely aware my feet are moving toward the exit. I can't discern how the interview went, and I'm nervous that I blew the questions. Who wants a teacher that can't escape her own feelings of self-loathing? What kind of help can I be?

I leave the school and drive two blocks to Mugs. A caramel mocha doesn't seem the smartest remedy for my already caffeine-addled mind, but I need something satisfying while I process my conversation with Mrs. Tunney.

I lumber into the shop, thankful my former principal didn't ask me how I feel about serving fancy coffees to teens. The place is full of young people and the noise level is high. Out of the corner of my eye I notice Jade standing with a couple girls.

Whether she spots me or not, she turns closer to the group, her back to me. *Lord, do I have to speak to her? I know what I said in the interview, but do I have to connect right now?* The sense I feel to speak to her grows as I order my drink. She's still there when I have the cup in my hands, so I trudge over to her.

"Jade, hi."

She flinches when I touch her shoulder, but she doesn't turn. "Hey."

The two girls with heavy eye makeup focus on me. "Hello, I'm Sabrina Wayson. Jade's a friend."

The two exchange suspicious looks. "From where?"

Jade shifts so she's facing all of us.

I speak before she does. "Church."

The two girls open their mouths, but no words come out.

The awkward level is as high as the carbs in my drink. "I just got done with a job interview. It's at your school."

All their eyes widen, but at least Jade speaks. "For real?"

I shrug. "I don't know if I got the job, though."

Their shoulders relax, and that does nothing to my confidence.

"Would it be a good thing if I ended up as a long-term sub at your school?"

If we were in a department store, I'd think the girls were mannequins. Jade takes her time, but responds. "I don't know. Can I get back to you?"

With that ringing endorsement, I excuse myself and nurse my drink all the way home. I have no idea how the interview went, if I'll get the job, and thanks to my chat with those girls, I'm not sure I even want Mrs. Tunney to hire me.

CHAPTER ELEVEN
HAYLEY

With one eye open, I fumble with my phone until I push snooze. First day of school and I have no motivation. Thanks to my mom and online shopping, I at least have some new clothes. But nothing that resembles what the other kids will be wearing.

Mom opens the door with such enthusiasm it ricochets off the wall and swings back. "Happy first day of school! Who's ready for junior high?"

I pull the covers over my head. "Not me."

She chuckles and rips the covers off me. "I know you're nervous, Hayley, but perspective is everything. Go in with a great attitude, and it will be an amazing day. Enter the halls with a negative mindset, and you will fulfill your own expectations."

I sit up and wipe my eyes. "Sounds like you speak from experience."

Mom plays with a loose thread on my comforter. "I do. I was so intimidated by art class that I would have an upset stomach every week when I knew I had to go. The teacher was critical, even made fun of my work. She told me to hide it for open house so my parents wouldn't see it."

Now I'm wide awake. "That's terrible!"

"It's hard enough when kids are mean, but for teachers to be so careless with words, it made those years that much more difficult. I didn't talk about it or ask for help, I sulked. Whined. Tried everything to get out of that class."

"What happened?"

"I got a 'D' in art and was given the nickname Eeyore. No one knew my pain, so they just thought I was annoying."

"What if I have a teacher like you did?"

She pats my knee. "You come to me and we will deal with it. The same answer if another student is being harsh."

What if they are cruel outside of class? Jade's too sneaky to get caught in school. "Thanks, Mom. I should get dressed."

"Of course." Her steps are tentative as she makes her way to the door. "Hayley, it's going to be a great year. I really believe that."

That makes one of us.

By third period, my hope that the year won't be terrible slightly improves. Jazmin and I share the same homeroom, and Bethany and I are in second period math together. My on-and-off again crush since pre-school, Seth Daniels, sits ahead of me in science. I can think of worse things.

Mrs. Franks starts with attendance, and I don't pay a lot of attention since Atkinson is usually the first name. My focus is Seth, hoping he's great with numbers so he can tutor me.

"Jade Green?"

Mrs. Franks question hangs in the air and I sit up, fully alert. "Jade? Are you here?"

I close my eyes. Goodbye great year.

Jade saunters in and snaps her gum as she hands the teacher a slip of paper.

"Welcome. You can have a seat across from Seth Daniels."

No, this can't be happening.

Jade nods and trudges over. Her smile is wide as she looks Seth's way, but when our eyes connect, her face contorts. "Hayley. Is that outfit from your mom?"

I narrow my eyes, too angry to back down. "No, I got it from yours."

Seth turns around, new metal braces in full display. "Wow. Got some aloe, Jade?"

She returns her attention to him. "No, why?"

He laughs. "You got burned by Hayley."

I cross my arms, feeling pretty proud of myself despite Mrs. Franks clearing her throat and glaring in our direction. Maybe this is the answer to surviving junior high. Instead of running away, come back twice as hard with sarcasm. After all, Jade's sitting at her desk, facing the teacher, quiet.

It's a first-day-of-school miracle.

After class, I fight the crowds to reach my locker. Seth's nearby with his friends. "Dude, math was awesome. Jade came in with attitude and Hayley gave it back to her without batting her eyelashes. I never saw Jade close her mouth so fast."

I bend down in my locker to grab my lunch, but my smile is wide.

"Who's Hayley?"

Seth sighs. "You know her, Hayley Atkinson. She's been in our class since pre-k."

There are mumbles followed by locker slams. "Oh, I know. Hangs out with Bethany and Jazmin?"

Seth's voice cracks. "Yeah, that's her."

"Interesting. The chubby girl fights back."

The crowd of laughter trails down the hall as I drop my lunch and wipe away hot tears. Remembering my new vow to make sarcasm my strategy, I take a breath to compose myself, slam the locker, and head to my next class. With every stomp I pray that one of those boys will be in Language Arts so I can have the last laugh.

There are so many comebacks running through my mind that when I stalk through the door, I don't notice the teacher or who's sitting where. I want to find laughing guys. It's all I have to go on, unless Seth's in the same class and tells me.

"Hayley, welcome to Language Arts."

I swivel and find the teacher with a wide smile, disarming all my anger. "Sabrina? You're my teacher?"

CHAPTER TWELVE
SABRINA

My first day of morning classes brings about one hundred students with names I need to memorize. It's a treat when Hayley enters before lunch. Just seeing someone familiar calms my nerves. "I'm the long-term sub. I was hired last week, so I had to work fast to get the room together. What do you think?"

I turn and point to the cream walls adorned with colorful grammar posters, as well as motivational pictures with various NFL players.

Hayley glances around the room, but she doesn't seem focused on the walls. "It's good. Do we sit where we want?" Her eyes appear to rest on a group of boys laughing and nudging each other.

"For now. I might create a seating chart once I get to know everyone."

Hayley nods and hustles over to the area where the guys are, throwing her backpack down with a thud. They stop the laughter for a moment, looking at Hayley, her bag, and then to a boy I assume is their leader. He shakes his head, and they sober, sitting down, eyes forward.

Looks like this class is going to double as drama.

By the end of the school day, I'm tempted to take my heels off and walk the halls in bare feet. Thankfully my classes were full of activity, but nothing emotionally taxing. Even having Jade in last period wasn't an issue.

Mrs. Tunney greets me in my doorway. "Coming back tomorrow?"

I reach for my oversized tote and chuckle. "So far, so good. Thank you again for believing in me."

She hands me a folder. "More paperwork to fill out. Sabrina, it doesn't take effort to believe in you. You were an amazing student, and the interview was excellent. Our hope is this is an outstanding experience, and that you will have a permanent job soon."

I stuff the folder in my bag and walk down the hall with her. A cluster of students remains, including the boys Hayley sat by. Something's amusing them, because their snickers and noise level increases.

"Seth, c'mon. That girl needs to be stopped."

I slow my steps and put my hand on the folder. "Mrs. Tunney, thanks for everything. I'll see you tomorrow." I wave her off, and drop the oversized envelope on the floor, so I can stay close to the taunts and reaction.

"Guys, Hayley heard you call her chubby. She lashed out at you because you deserved it. Besides, it was as funny as what she said to Jade. I give her props for comedic timing."

It takes me longer than necessary to pick the envelope up so I can hear the rest of their debate.

"She made us look stupid."

The Seth kid throws his gym bag over his shoulder. "No, you did that by yourselves. We have practice. I don't want to be late."

They follow his lead and jog down the hall, leaving me alone with nothing but worry for Hayley.

The other teachers warned me that the first week of school would deplete me of all energy by Wednesday. Before the last bell rings on hump day, I count the minutes until I can get my hands on a cup of coffee.

As I work on leaving the building, Bethany comes alongside with a big grin. "Hey, Miss Wayson. Are you going to Linked tonight? Are you bringing frappes? Jazmin wants to know if there will be pizza."

Oops. With the new job, I forgot about the rest of my schedule. Like Linked. "As fast as you're talking, it sounds like caffeine is the last thing you need."

She throws her head back with a laugh. "Funny. You're joking, right? We're kind of addicted to those drinks."

I push on the front doors, letting Bethy walk through first. "I'll bring some. Will Hayley be there?"

Bethany shrugs. "Not sure. I think so. Why?"

It's my turn to raise my shoulders. "I missed her at the last meeting is all."

"Gotcha. Well, my dad's here, so I'll see you tonight. Don't forget."

I roll my eyes. "I know, don't come without your fancy coffees."

When I return home, there's not a lot of time for me to unwind. I make a sandwich, change clothes, and correct second period papers before I leave for the coffee shop. When I arrive, Vanessa and Kane are working. She sees me first. "Look who's here--the new teacher."

"Who still works a shift on Saturdays. I haven't completely abandoned you." I slide onto a stool. "I'll take six iced mochas."

Kane ducks into our chat. "Whoa. School must be wearing you out."

I pull out my credit card. "It is, but these are for the Linked ladies and teens. You remember that ministry, right?"

Kane shakes his head and starts making one of the drinks. "I rarely listen to any of your and Vanessa's chatter."

Vanessa rings the transaction. "Don't listen to him. He lives for our conversation."

Before he has a chance to reply, I feel a tap on my shoulder.

Charlie. "I see more of you here than in our development. Are you on a break at school?"

He nods and stifles a yawn. "Yeah, huge paper due tomorrow. Speaking of, did you get that job?"

Kane hands me a carrier full of drinks, and I lift it by the bottom to ready for my exit. "I did. Can you believe I'm back in our old school?"

Charlie flashes a smile. "That has to feel weird. Do you need assistance?" He nods toward the drinks. "I can help you get them to your car, if you like."

"No, you're in line. I've got it, but thanks. I'll be praying for you and your paper."

He keeps his gaze on me. "Appreciate it. And Sabrina?"

I stop, feeling the ice in the drinks jiggle. "Yeah?"

"Congratulations. Any school would be blessed to have you."

I'm pretty sure the ice melts before I reach my car. My dreamy smile stays, until I enter Linked and see Hayley with arms folded, scowling.

CHAPTER THIRTEEN
HAYLEY

The bright pink and black accents in the newly painted Linked room don't help my lack of motivation. Not even Sabrina's warm smile and tray of drinks topped with whipped cream deliciousness brighten my spirits. In fact, seeing my Linked mentor who is also my temporary teacher only enhances my miserable state.

Sabrina approaches me first. "Hayley, long time, no see. Ready for some caffeine?"

I shrug. "I guess. Thanks." I reach for the one closest to me and take a sip.

She doesn't move. "Everything going okay with your first week at school?"

Let's see. After I made fun of Jade and Seth's friends with my sarcastic approach, they teamed up and are working to humiliate me. By the grace of God and their collective love for Seth, he stopped Jade from tripping me and the boys messing with my locker. Yeah, I'm having a blast.

Jade leaves her seat and grabs an iced drink. "Hayley thinks she's the class comedian this year."

Lena, Mrs. Cheri, and Sabrina exchange looks that include furrowed brows. Jade could interpret the chat in a number of directions. Sabrina takes her bait. "How so? I think all of you have a strong sense of humor, among other positive traits."

Jade pulls her phone out and stares at the screen while she blabs to the women. "I didn't say I agree with Hayley. She's just become the queen of sarcasm." She looks up and lasers in on me. "It's not pretty."

Mrs. Cheri gasps as I try not to squeeze my cup too hard to avoid an iced coffee explosion.

Jazmin clears her throat. "Speaking of pretty, did anyone look at my nail polish?"

Bethany glances around the table, and then to Jazmin's hands. "You're right. They look beautiful. Hayley, wouldn't you agree?" Her voice sounds strained.

"Sure. Of course, Jazmin always looks amazing."

Mrs. Cheri lets out some air and stands. "Well, who needs an icebreaker when we have a lively conversation taking place? Girls, I'm glad you feel comfortable enough to share so honestly. I love how you're able to build each other up with positive words like admiring Jazmin's nail polish. That's our goal here."

Lena chuckles. "To have awesome nail polish?"

We all giggle as Mrs. Cheri continues. "We can work on that, too. But words are important, and that's what we're going to talk about tonight."

I slide down in my seat. That doesn't sound fun to me.

Mrs. Cheri takes out several tubes of toothpaste and passes them around so we each have one.

Bethany holds hers up, a green mint kind I don't like. "Are we going to brush our teeth?"

Mrs. Cheri walks to the front of the table. "Make sure each of you have a paper towel and a handful of toothpicks. You can open your toothpaste and place the tube on the towel."

Sabrina helps Mrs. Cheri by taking out paper towels and tooth picks. "I think I know what we're about to do. It's good. You'll like this."

Jade plugs her nose. "I hate bubble gum flavor."

Mine is the kind we use at home, the white kind with baking soda. What's Mrs. Cheri's plan?

"Hate's a strong word for toothpaste. It's a strong word for a lot of things. That's what brings me to our activity. Take your tube, and squeeze a good amount on your paper towel."

Jazmin grabs her bottle by the middle and pumps it. Green and white goo oozes out. "Okay, Mrs. Cheri. I have no idea where you're going with this."

Lena follows the rest of us. "It smells minty in here."

My glop is in the shape of ice cream on a cone.

Mrs. Cheri holds a toothpick. "Okay, now I want you to take your toothpick and put the toothpaste back in the tube. All of it."

We focus on our pastor's wife. Bethany speaks first. "There's no way."

I nod. "Bethy's right. We can't get that back in the tube."

Jade shrugs. "I'm going to try. I didn't pour out a lot."

I scrape as much paste as I can and attempt to plug it back in the tube. More stays on the cap than back in the hole. Glancing around, I see no one is having success.

After a couple minutes of quiet work, Mrs. Cheri sits down. "Toothpicks down. Now, let's see how we did. Anyone get it all back in?"

Jade has her toothpick still in her hand, shoving paste in the miniscule tube opening. "I'm close."

Our leader smiles. "Ah, but I said all, not most of it. Anyone?"

My paper towel looks as if a toddler tried to brush their teeth without supervision.

"Any thoughts on why we did this tonight?" Mrs. Cheri glances around.

Sabrina looks up. "Trying to return that to the tube is as successful as trying to take back words we've said."

My heart pangs as my throat tightens.

Bethany's jaw lowers, then she shakes her head. "That. Is. Powerful."

Lena stares at her mess on the table. "Wow. I never thought of it that way. Did you, Hayley? Jazmin? Jade?"

A long stretch of silence and reflection covers the room before I speak. "Sometimes my words just tumble out. When I'm mad, I blurt the first thing that comes to mind."

Sabrina raises her hand. "I'm guilty of that, too."

Bethany sighs. "We probably all are."

I steal a peek at Jade, who is tearing small pieces off clean parts of her towel.

Mrs. Cheri folds her hands. "I think you're right, Bethy. If we keep the conversation here, it becomes a cool object lesson. I'd like us to take this topic a step further. What do we do to avoid situations like Hayley described? How can we not blurt out the first thing we think of when we talk?"

My mind races to find the church-y answers leaders want to hear, but Jazmin beats me to it. "Pray. My parents start our day that way, and even ask Jesus to help us guard our hearts---and what spills out of our mouths."

Sabrina collects the paper towels. "That's great, but you said your parents pray. Do you?"

Jazmin bites her lip. "Not really."

Mrs. Cheri pats her on the arm. "It's okay, we're here to learn together. This is something Pastor Chet and I still encourage Sabrina with. We want her to have her own faith, not lean on our beliefs or prayers. Just because she sits with me at church each week and lives in a pastor's house doesn't mean she's a friend of Jesus or promised eternity in heaven."

"Mom's right. Another thing that helps me is praying the armor of God from Ephesians six every morning. When I ask God to protect my thoughts with the helmet of salvation, it gives me a fast track to having the sense to say the right thing, even when I'm angry."

How many times have I prayed this week? Zero.

Mrs. Cheri leans her arms on the table. "Girls, I don't want to see you living in regret because you put words out there that you can't take back. Junior high is hard. You should have each other's back."

I don't look at Jade, I don't say anything. My stomach is tight and my forehead feels wet. My throat is dry. I know the ladies are right. I haven't been positive about anything except revenge.

It's time to dump the mockery strategy and give prayer a try. Because sarcasm sure isn't working for me.

You're Beautiful

CHAPTER FOURTEEN
SABRINA

My first teaching paycheck's in the bank, so I invite Lena to join me for coffee before my own barista shift starts. I realize I haven't been out with anyone close to my age in months, and when she left church the other night with her kids, she looked exhausted. Thankfully, her mom agreed to babysit so we could enjoy our time together.

Lena, wearing a tunic with red print leggings, greets me with a warm hug and bright smile. "Thank you for inviting me. I can't tell you when I've been out without kids that didn't involve going to the bank or getting groceries."

I chuckle, a little nervous titter blended in. She doesn't quite make me want to sign up for motherhood. "I'm glad you could join me. I thought since we both serve in Linked that it would make sense to get to know one another. It's not every day there are volunteers signing up to work with junior high school girls."

Lena scuffs her foot against the wooden flooring. "How about you? You also work with them. In fact, I thought that was your coffee job, too, at Mugs?"

I grimace at the thought of being at the teen hangout. "Oh, no. I don't have the energy for that. This is the adult crowd. Customers are a little artsy sometimes, but everyone is very nice. Go ahead and order, today's on me. My treat."

Is that a tear in her eye?

"Sabrina, you are a blessing. Thank you. I've got a sweet tooth today." She turns to Kane, who's at the counter ready to take our drink selections. "How about a hot mocha with half a pump of caramel?"

He nods, and I order the same. After I pay, we stand to the side, waiting for our drinks. I take a breath, not sure what to say, when she turns to me. "How do you like teaching?"

I'm sure my eyes light up like a New Year's Eve ball. "I'm adjusting, but I love it. I'm going to miss them when it's time to leave."

"Do you see all the Linked girls?"

I nod, reaching for napkins. "They all have my class, but not all at the same time. Jade and Hayley are together, though."

Kane places our cups down near me, and I pick them up as Lena finds a booth and sits. I hand her the drink and take a seat. Lena holds the cup as if she's using it to warm her hands. "How does that go, with Jade and Hayley?"

I feel the heat from my cup and decide to wait before taking a sip. "It was pretty much like our meetings. Since the last one, I have noticed a change in Hayley. She seems to be finding things to encourage Jade about. When Jade's in a bad mood, it takes creativity, but Hayley's really trying."

Lena's cocoa-colored eyes widen. "Praise God. Maybe that toothpaste object lesson reached her."

"I know it did me, I've been watching what I say ever since."

Before Lena can reply, the door opens and a breeze enters, blowing the wind chimes Kane hung inside. Charlie steps in, waves, and heads right for us.

"Hey, Charlie. What brings you by?"

He grins. "Caffeine. What else? Funny seeing you as a customer."

I shift so I can see both Lena and Charlie. "Not for too long. My shift starts later. Charlie, this is my friend, Lena. Lena, this is my friend and neighbor, Charlie."

The two exchange pleasantries while I sip my mocha.

Lena focuses on Charlie. "Did you want to sit with us?"

He shakes his head, a mass of curls that need a trim. "I couldn't. It looks like a great girl time for you both."

She rolls her eyes. "Nonsense. You can help me get to know Sabrina better. It sounds like you've seen her more than I have. Sabrina, move over and let Charlie sit by you.:

I raise an eyebrow at her, but she continues smiling. "Of course."

Lena keeps going. "Okay, so tell me all about Sabrina. I know her from church, and that she works here and at school. That's it. Fill in the blanks."

I start to open my mouth, but she holds up a hand. "I want to hear from Charlie, first."

Okay, then.

He slides his coat off and moves an inch closer. I'm very aware he's close. I also realize I don't mind it, but I'm nervous in front of the guy I've known sixteen years.

"What to say about Sabrina." He grins and shoots a glance my way. "She's the best. You definitely want her on your team if you play wiffleball, that was the neighborhood game when we were younger. She's a fierce protector. I watched her tell off a bully from another street who was picking on another girl. Sabrina's smarter than she gives herself credit for. I don't need to see her in the classroom to know she's an excellent teacher." He pauses, his eyes brightening. "She's also beautiful. It's not just the long blonde hair, but the glow she has that I know starts from her heart."

Lena's voice softens as she considers his words. "Charlie, that's really a wonderful sentiment."

I want to reply, but my eyes fill. Besides my parents, no one has said anything that encouraging or amazing before. How can he see a different girl than the one my biological dad mouths off about? My throat feels like I swallowed a rock. "Charlie, I didn't even pay you to say that."

Charlie doesn't smile. "Sabrina, you wouldn't need to." He stands, and reaches for his coat. "I have to go. It was nice to meet you, Lena."

Her smile looks like she's met her favorite rock star. "Same here."

Charlie focuses on me. "I pray that one day you will see yourself the way everyone else does. You're pretty awesome, Sabrina Wayson." With that, he takes his drink, waves, and exits out the door.

Lena leans in. "What was that?"

I shrug. "I know, right? That's a lot of compliments for a neighbor I only see here every once in a while."

She rolls her eyes and takes a drink. "Sabrina." Something tells me her tone of voice is one she's used on her kids. "Has he been coming around a lot?"

I bite my lip, trying to remember. "Kane mentioned he stops in late afternoon sometimes but doesn't always order."

Her volume increases. "Sabrina! My kids can connect dots better than you can."

"What do you mean? He's a friend, he loves the coffee here."

Lena shakes her head. "You're impossible. He visits during after school hours, wondering if you are working. He came today, a weekend, and you are working later. I asked to describe you and he gave the most beautiful tribute I've ever heard. That man likes you, and I don't mean as a neighbor."

CHAPTER FIFTEEN
HAYLEY

I'm not sure who had the idea to partner our school with the community health center's pool for a Phys Ed rotation, but as leaves change and temps drop, I have to start packing my swim suit and towel for school. It's a torture reserved for middle school, and of course, Jazmin and Bethany aren't in my class.

But Jade is.

I climb the bus steps looking for a friendly face. Ava Benson, a quiet girl who lives a block away, smiles. "Hey, Ava. Can I sit with you?"

She moves over. "Nothing like a field trip to the pool in October, right?"

I throw my bag down at my feet and sigh. "Worst idea ever."

Ava chuckles. "I don't think anyone thought this through. I have to wear a cap or my hair looks like one of the 'before' pictures in a magazine ad. And I'm sure no one will make fun of me for that attractive accessory." Her giggle continues.

I never thought about the hair issue. For me, I pull it back in a ponytail and let it dry. It's not that easy for everyone. Ava doesn't seem too bothered by the possibility of getting picked on. "I promise I won't. I know what teasing feels like, and I wouldn't do it to someone else. At least, not anymore."

She sits up as the bus starts for the health center a couple miles away. "What do you mean? Did you used to bully people? I always thought you were nice."

"I think I am, but I was hurting because of words being said to me."

Ava shifts in her seat. "Do you mind telling me more?"

I turn around to see if it's safe to talk. Jade's in the back with the popular crowd. "I was told I was ugly. Not just ugly, but she said 'pretty ugly.' I think it would have hurt less to have been kicked. It's all I could think about, and I went from avoiding going out to wanting revenge."

The bus is at the last intersection before the destination. Ava glances around the bus. "I have one more question."

"Sure. What?"

"Did Jade say those things?"

The wind feels knocked out of me. The bus comes to a stop and the door opens. We stand and Ava grabs her gear. "It's okay, Hayley. She's said stuff to me, too. Thing is, none of what she said is true. Not about me, nor about you."

It's my turn to exit the bus, but I can barely put one foot in front of the other. Jade bullied Ava? And it didn't bother her?

We walk into the locker room and pick out a place to store our things. I find a place near Ava. "Did you mean what you said on the bus? I mean, you have looked at me, right?"

She rolls her eyes. "What? You want to look like all the girls on your favorite show? Can you tell them apart? I'd rather stand out. Sure, my hair needs a swimming cap and extra attention, but people remember me. For my unique look. My nice words. Nothing cookie cutter about me."

Ava's confidence in the middle of the locker room amazes me.

"Wow. Where were you over the summer?"

Her laughter rings through the bland changing room. "Hayley, I was swimming with my cap on."

After forty minutes of improving our dives, we dress and return to school. I have two minutes to walk down the hall for science when I hear a bunch of girls laughing. I'm still not confident enough to turn around in case the victim is me, but it doesn't take long for them to pass me.

"Jade Green, I can't believe you don't know how to dive. All that time in the pool."

"I don't go to the pool to be an Olympian. I go to layout. Duh."

"But, Jade, you looked like you were dancing off that board."

"Yeah, and not a good dancer."

I didn't dare to attempt eye contact, but I know the group. The eighth-grade cheerleaders. Carlie Riggs pauses, causing all the girls to freeze before hitting her. I slow my pace. "Jade, maybe you should take a break today."

Jade faces Carlie, the ringleader. "What do you mean, a break?"

"Like, find another group to hang with. We're about class and style. You---" Carlie's disdain shows all over her face. "Aren't." With that, the girls giggle and move on, leaving Jade in the middle of the hall.

"Fine. Whatever. I don't need any of you." Jade's voice tries to come off strong. She falters at the end, but her words manage to hit me right in the gut. Everything in me wants to keep walking to science. My vow to improve my attitude and words forces me to stop next to her.

"Hey, Jade. You okay?"

She glances at me and starts to narrow her eyes and speak, but stops. "I've had better days."

Now what? I'm not prepared for her to be nice. "Did you want to talk?"

Jade shrugs and returns to a crawl-like pace. "Not much to say. Rejection stinks."

"It's the worst."

She stops again, staring at me for a few seconds before speaking. "Do you want to go to Mugs after school?"

Panic slams my stomach as soon as I hear 'Mugs.' "Um, are you sure?"

"Why wouldn't I be?"

"Jade, you told me months ago not to go there because I didn't belong."

Her mouth opens wide enough for flies to enter. "I said that?"

I nod, afraid to speak.

"And you didn't go? For months?"

Another affirmative.

The bell rings, but we don't move despite the empty hallway. She sighs. "I'm sorry, Hayley. That was pretty rotten of me. I have no idea what I said or why. My mom said I can be brutal sometimes. If you don't want to go, I get it."

"I'd like that. I'll text my mom after school to make sure it's okay."

Jade's smile is as warm as a campfire in July. "Great. Thanks, Hayley."

I open the door to science and take my seat, trying to process it all. I think God just blessed me with a miracle.

CHAPTER SIXTEEN
SABRINA

The text is so sweet and simple I want to screenshot, print, and frame it.

Sabrina, can we get together? I need to talk to someone smart. Hayley

After a week of lower-than-average quiz grades, drama with third period, and the sixth-period boys stinking up the room with their body odor, her message is a balm to my tired soul. We decide to meet at my coffee shop Saturday morning.

Hayley strolls in with a smile, along with a long blue sweater and black leggings. Her long brown hair is in braids, and if possible, her grin widens when she notices me and waves. I jump up and give her a hug.

"Thanks, Sabrina, for meeting with me. I'm sure you're sick of seventh graders by now."

I dismiss the thought with my hand and gesture for her to sit. "Long week, but I'm always thrilled to hear from you. Did you want anything before we chat? My treat."

She glances to the counter. "Are your mochas as good as the ones they make at Mugs?"

I shrug. "Why don't you find out? Go ahead and order."

Hayley leans her arms on the table, her eyes wide. "Are you allowed to make it?"

Kane's at the counter and it's pretty quiet as far as customers go. I don't work until next Saturday, but it's worth asking. "Be right back." I scoot over to Kane, ask if it's okay, and he nods. I call her over.

In three minutes, Hayley is walking back to her seat with a steaming mug of mocha, topped off with whipped cream and a squirt of chocolate and caramel syrup. She spoons some of the white cream and takes her time placing it in her mouth, eyes closed. "This part is fantastic."

I roll my eyes. "You didn't even get to the drink yet, silly. Hurry up so we can talk."

She pushes the mug back a little. "I'll chat while this cools. I wanted to tell you that I had a miracle this week. I don't know what to make of it."

I sip my latte. "I'm happy to help if I can."

Hayley takes a deep breath. "I overheard a bunch of girls making fun of Jade. I knew it bothered her. She tried to pretend that it didn't, but we started talking. She even asked if I'd want to go to Mugs with her sometime."

Color me surprised. "Hayley, that's fantastic. You were able to reach out and make a difference. Praise God."

"Thing is, a few months ago, she made fun of me there. It really hurt, and I took what she said seriously. So much so, I haven't been back."

There's a stab to my gut, and I'm pretty sure it's not the latte. "I'm sorry to hear that."

"I told Jade, and she doesn't even remember saying it. She apologized. Thing is, since she was mean to me that time, I haven't been able to forget. I believe what she said, even if she doesn't recall the whole thing."

Instantly my mind takes me back to the mall when I saw my biological dad, when he'd made it clear my looks made me unworthy of a man. "Hayley, you know those words aren't true. You know where they really came from, right?"

She takes a drink, and furrows her brow. "Jade?"

I shake my head. "No. The devil is the real defeated one. But he works with limited resources, using the same old tricks to make us feel defeated. Lying is his go-to tactic, the one we always fall for. Whatever you heard that day is a lie. They aren't the promises of God."

She bites her lip for a moment. "Sabrina, take a look. I'm not a size zero or whatever the other girls are. I can't even shop at the same stores Bethany and Jazmin do. My teeth are crooked and my hair looks dry and…"

I put my hands up. "Girl, you need to stop. Who created you?"

Hayley shrugs. "My parents?"

With a chuckle, I continue. "God is our creator. When you put yourself down, you are telling God that He makes junk. Is that what you think?"

She shakes her head. "No. But I don't feel pretty. I feel what Jade said. Pretty ugly."

I flinch and reach over to squeeze Hayley's hand. "That isn't true. Not one word of it. You know what my parents call that kind of talk? Stinkin' Thinkin'. It's negative and it has nothing to do with the promises of God."

"What does God think of me?"

It's my turn to offer a wide smile. "Oh, Hayley. You are a masterpiece to Him. We are the last of His Creation, apart from rest. We aren't an afterthought, we were given such intricate beautiful thought that we were created last. We are His beloved daughters. With Jesus as the King of Kings, we're His royal princesses."

Hayley sits back. "I never thought of myself as a princess."

"Well, it's true. The question is, are you going to live like you believe it, or keep receiving the lies?"

"Sabrina, I've been miserable all these months. Even my thoughts became ugly. I don't want to live that way."

Another image of my first dad. His addiction, his actions, his words are all ugly. But he's not. Neither am I. "If Jade asked you to Mugs, I think you should go. Walk in there with your head held high. You belong there as much as anyone else."

She swiped the corner of her eye. "What if I go there and Jade's mean? What if she never meant the nice things she said the other day?"

"It's a risk, I know. If that were to happen, and I doubt it will, the truth stands. You are beautiful. You have amazing purpose. You are royalty, and unless you allow it, nothing and nobody can change that."

Her grin is back. "Thank you. I know I kind of blew you off, and everyone at Linked. I didn't mean to."

I think back to my own attempt to skip a meeting because my wound was so gaping. "Now you know to come to us. Let us help and pray for you."

She nods. "I will. I promise. I have one more question."

I take another sip. "Anything."

"Do you have a pop quiz planned for Monday?"

CHAPTER SEVENTEEN
HAYLEY

There aren't butterflies in my stomach, I'm positive there's a nest of angry bees looking for their stolen honey. The door to Mugs feels like lead, but I use both hands and push. When it opens, I shuffle until I'm fully inside. Glancing around while I swallow hard, I don't see anyone I know.

"Hayley, over here!"

I turn toward the voice and find Jade sitting in a booth, waving. The breath I expel is nearly a sob because I've held so much in, afraid this was going to be a joke. My feet feel lighter as I move toward the booth.

Jade pivots the menu so it's facing me. "I got here a little early because my mom wanted to drop me off before she got groceries."

I try to find my voice. "No problem. Did you order anything?"

She shakes her head. "I wasn't sure what you'd want."

"What do you usually get when you sit with the ninth graders?"

Jade rolls her eyes. "They order for me. It's a really long name with skinny in it and it tastes like funny water. C'mon, let's order something fun."

She jumps up and reaches for my arm as we jog together toward the counter. My heartbeat seems a normal rhythm; I don't feel as warm as I did when I entered. This might be fun after all.

We order two pumpkin spice lattes and Jade opens her wallet. "My mom gave me money. My treat."

I reach for napkins. "Wow. Thanks, Jade."

As we return to our booth, out of the corner of my eye I see the ninth-grade cheerleaders Jade often hangs with bouncing in, full of giggles. I slide down in my seat, sure this outing is going to take a negative turn.

Jade leans toward her drink and inhales. "If fall has a smell, I think this is it."

I glance at the cheerleaders, now at the counter. Doesn't Jade see them? "You should try Sabrina's creation. She makes an amazing mocha."

Jade rolls her eyes. "Hopefully better than the test she created for us. That was a beast."

The cheerleaders move as a cohesive unit our way. "How do you think you did?"

She shrugs. "Probably failed it. I didn't study. I thought I'd remember what I read in my notes. Turns out, I didn't."

The girls move past us, not saying a word. I realize I'm holding my breath again. "I studied and I still don't think I passed. It was hard."

Jade nods, sipping the pumpkin beverage.

"You know, if you want to sit with them, you can. I get it."

She scrunches her nose. "Sit with who?"

"The ninth-grade cheerleaders. They just walked past us."

Jade swivels around, and almost as quickly, turns back and focuses on me. "Hayley, I said I was sorry. I promise I won't ditch you or say mean things. I really am trying not to be so harsh."

Another exhale, and then I wipe my damp hands on my pants. "We've had a rocky time through the years, and I don't want to say something dumb and make you regret coming here to meet me."

Jade places a spoon in her ceramic mug and stirs for a moment before speaking. "Hayley, did you ever think that I'm anxious? I might not remember every mean thing I've said, but I'm aware I haven't been the nicest person. You aren't the only one. I've mouthed off to my parents and teachers, too. Other kids. Like I said, I'm working to be better. But every time I'm around someone I've been a brat to, I'm afraid they will get revenge. Because I deserve it."

I shake my head. "Do you read the Bible at all?"

80

She makes a sound that I can't identify, but if smirk has an utterance, that was it. "Not really."

"I know, you think it's lame. Mrs. Cheri showed me an app where I can read and it doesn't take long. I even understand what it says, and it helps a lot. I learned last week that we all fall short, mess up. Thing is, Jesus gives us grace."

"Grace? Like what we say at dinner?"

I giggle. "Not exactly. Grace is something like Sabrina giving us that test, and say we really did fail. But imagine if she returned it to us and she gave herself the failing grade, and gave us an 'A.'"

Jade's mouth drops. "No way. We couldn't get an A."

"Not without help, and Sabrina sacrificed herself. She failed her work to give us perfection. The reading said that grace is favor we don't deserve."

"What does that have to do with me?"

I definitely need another sip to soothe my dry throat. "I won't get revenge. Instead, I'd like for us to try to be friends. Real friends, not one day we get along, and the next, we avoid each other or say nasty things. I could even be your accountability partner. Pastor Chet talked about that once. It's where someone meets with you, maybe once a week, to see how you're doing with something you're struggling with."

She slowly nods. "You would check and see how nice I'm being?"

"Yeah. And if you're not doing well, I'd encourage you. I could even pray with you."

Jade fidgets with the spoon. "It sounds hard."

I think about me trying to picture myself dropping every thought I have about being ugly to the feet of Jesus so He can take care of it and instead put the truth about me in my mind. "Change isn't easy."

She sits up and smiles. "Can we try?"

CHAPTER EIGHTEEN
SABRINA

The lake effect snow machine is in full effect as I park in the school lot with the entire commute looking like someone flipped a snow globe upside down. My heart needs time to settle down after the low visibility travel. The good news about northeast Ohio, in ten minutes, the sun will be out and the snow will melt in time for students to trek in for their last day before Thanksgiving break.

Mrs. Tunney greets me as soon as I close the door and wipe my feet on the lobby rug. "Sabrina, just the person I want to see. Do you have a minute?"

My racing heart doesn't have a chance to rest. "Sure. Everything okay?"

I don't hear her response, but notice her hand gesture for me to follow her. Within moments, we're in her office. She offers the seat across from her.

"Thanks for seeing me on short notice. I know students will be arriving soon, so I'll keep this short. You've done a wonderful job in the junior high department. When I observed you in the classroom and I gave you feedback, you took a good job and made it great."

I fidget with my hands. Is this her kind goodbye as Mrs. Styles plans to make her return after the holidays? "Thank you. The kids are full of grace, and the other teachers have been very supportive. It's been a blessing."

She smiles and rests her elbows on her desk. "Are you interested in being here permanently?"

There's no way I just heard a job offer. "But---I'm here for Mrs. Styles. She's---"

Mrs. Tunney's phone beeps. She glances at it, but returns her focus to me. "Mrs. Styles resigned. She's going to stay home full-time with Cole. I'm pleased with your performance, and we try to hire alumni. The job is yours if you'd like it."

Please don't cry. You have mascara on. "It would be an honor."

If I could dance down the hall and to my classroom, I would. Jazmin waves as I near her locker. "Good morning, Jazmin. Did you have any trouble getting to school with that burst of snow?"

She gathers her books and shuts the door. "No, but my mom's determined. She knows I'm home from school the rest of the week. I was going to be here even if Mrs. Tunney closed the place."

I chuckle and follow her inside the room. "Believe it or not, even my parents were excited when vacations ended and I had to go back to school."

Jazmin laughs. "I can't picture Pastor Chet and Mrs. Cheri anxious to get rid of you. You're like, amazing."

"You're too kind, Jazmin. I can say this, I'm blessed."

She stands next to her desk, but hesitates before sitting down, her eyebrows raised. "Care to share?"

Only Jazmin would have the courage to pry. And succeed. "I'm no longer a long-term sub. Mrs. Tunney offered me the job. Mrs. Styles isn't returning."

Jazmin's grin starts small, and then like the sunrise, it eclipses everything as she runs over to me and gives me a hug. "You're wrong, though."

"About what?"

She walks back to her desk and sits down. "It's us who are blessed."

My parents are in the living room, standing, as I come home. My goal is to tell them about the job and take them to dinner, but seeing them face the door as if they are waiting for me is definitely not the norm for them.

I take my coat off and hang it, and place my purse on the same hook. "Everything okay? You look kind of serious."

Dad steps toward me. "We do need to share something with you."

I sit in the chair next to the couch, where they park on the very edge. "Great. I have news, too."

Mom picks imaginary lint off her sweater, so now I'm certain the chat isn't going to be pleasant. "It's about Thanksgiving."

"They ran out of turkey?"

No one cracks a smile.

Dad continues. "My brother wants to join us for dinner. I haven't given him an answer, though."

Dread fills me from top to bottom. "My father? Since when does he want to be included in Wayson events?"

He shrugs. "He visited my office today. Although he did ask for money, he also was asking questions about rehab."

I crack my knuckles and expel a blast of hot air. "It's a scam. He'll never go. He just wants you to feel sorry for him and keep forking over your hard-earned money while he drinks it away."

Dad nods, his mouth in a flat line. "You might be right, Sabrina. We're a family, I wasn't going to reply without talking to you about it."

"He could come drunk. Or, not show up at all."

Mom nods hard enough that her hair bounces. "She's right."

I slowly breathe in as I process the scenarios. As I exhale, I realize there could be positives. "Maybe he's finally ready to change. Although, last time I saw him, that prayer request seemed far off from even turning into a praise."

Both of them level their gazes right into my eyes.

Dad starts first. "When did you see him?"

The wall clock ticks away the seconds as I attempt to find the words.

Mom's turn. "Sabrina, what's wrong?"

I sigh, praying I can have this conversation without tears. "Over the summer, I saw dad at the mall."

Her stare continues. "Did he approach you?"

I nod, and the ugly cry comes out like waterfalls.

Mom stands and I follow, running to her tender hug that she holds onto while I sob. When I feel the tears slowing down, I step back. Dad stands next to us, and rubs my back.

"We had small talk at the food court. He mentioned making better choices. That he found a rental place close to church. Then he made comments about my nose ring." A weepy sigh escapes. "And my singleness."

Mom's eyes narrow and her lips disappear into a thin, tight line. "Sabrina. Rod doesn't know you the way your Heavenly Father knows you, and His plans for you."

I'm not really up to the God's my ultimate Dad chat right now.

I wipe the corner of my eye with my sleeve. "I know, but he isn't wrong. All my friends have boyfriends. Not me. What's wrong with me?"

Dad's words are immediate and gripped with emotion. "Nothing. Absolutely nothing."

"Then why do his words pierce me?"

Mom sighs and offers for me to sit between them on the couch. "Perhaps it's a flaming arrow."

"Come again?"

Dad shifts in his seat. "Something the devil is lying to you about and hurling at you."

Sounds about right. I rub my temples. "Is it okay if I pray about Thanksgiving? I'm pretty overwhelmed."

Mom sits close enough to me that our legs touch. She squeezes my hand. "Absolutely. How about we take tonight and start planning the next Linked meeting?"

I look to Dad, and then Mom. The conversation, as short as it's been, depletes me of all energy. And faith. "I'd like to take a raincheck. I'd rather be alone and eat ice cream." My laugh is sarcastic. "I'll make all my father's thoughts about me come true."

Mom's tone is loving, but firm. "Sweetheart, if you do that, you're letting the lie and the liar win. Satan has limited resources and time. He's going to use what works. If he can make you feel defeated, it takes the reality of him being the true defeated one away."

"Mom, I don't know how I can clear my head and work on a ministry to encourage girls in Christ when I'm struggling."

She pats the top of my fist. "That's exactly what Linked is about. We're not looking for perfect mentors, but authentic ones. These girls need to know the devil's schemes and how to combat them."

I slowly inhale and take a moment before exhaling. "And, how do we?"

Dad interjects. "The Armor of God, sweetheart. Every day I prayed that over you, and my hope is you continue to do the same. The shield of faith extinguishes those flaming arrows, the things the devil throws at you to distract and discourage you. You know who you are, Sabrina Wayson. More importantly, you know whose you are. Don't let a wounded soul's comments take you down."

He's right. I also let daily prayer slip once college started. "Do you think the girls will be impacted by me and my struggles?"

Mom chuckles, her laugh as melodious as her singing. "Absolutely. They look up to you. If you enter that meeting with your head high and remind them they are made perfect, I am certain it will help them with the lies the enemy has been telling them."

I stand. "Thanks. When I first came home, I was so thankful and excited. Mrs. Tunney hired me on a permanent basis. Then, hearing about my father, I wondered if God even cared. Because of both of you taking the time to love me, I know God loves me, and whatever happens, He has my back."

The two exchange glances before Dad rises and offers a hug. "That's my girl. More importantly, you're God's girl. Now, before you two starts planning, how about we go out to dinner and celebrate Sabrina's great news?"

Mom looks to me, and leaves the couch. "Let me get my purse and jacket. Is it okay if I text everyone in Linked and ask that they pray for me?"

Dad stretches. "What kind of pastor would I be if I said no to that? We'll pray together tonight, too."

I pull out my phone and compose a text. *I need prayer for direction. Help a girl out?*

Barely ten seconds after I send, replies come in.

Bethany writes, *On it! Love you!*

Jazmin's next. *Of course!*

Jade's response surprises me. *Would you pray for me, too?*

Lena doesn't take long to reply. *You've got it, friend.*

Hayley's message arrives right after Lena's. *I will right now. God's got you, Sabrina!*

I look up to see my parents at the door. Dad opens it as we walk past. "By the sound of the phone going off, you've got a lot of prayer support."

I wait for him to head down the sidewalk so I can walk with him. "I already have a peace that before I go to bed, I know God will have the direction for us to take."

CHAPTER NINETEEN
HAYLEY

Bethany's eyes seem as big as frisbees coming at me when I share her the news the Tuesday before Thanksgiving. She holds up her hands. "Wait. You're telling me that Jade called you pretty ugly and said you should never go to Mugs? And you listened to her?"

Jazmin steps in between us. "Hold up. Not only all that, but then you two talk about it and become friends? And you are helping her by being her accountability partner?"

The two get up, staring, Jazmin tapping her foot.

My voice is more like a squeak. "Are you guys mad?"

Bethany shakes her head. "I'm not. I wish you would have told us back when she said those mean and untrue things. We could have helped."

Jazmin and Bethy are more like a tag team. When Bethany takes a breath, Jazmin jumps in. "It's awesome how you are checking in with Jade about her mood and words."

"It sounds weird, but that toothpaste talk we had at Linked, I couldn't get it out of my mind. She's opening up to me more. She's lonely a lot of the time. Do you think we could invite her to the mall tonight?"

The two exchange looks and answer yes in unison.

An hour later, we're at the mall buying smoothies when we spot Mrs. Cheri and Pastor Chet holding hands as they walk past the jewelry kiosk. She recognizes us and waves. "Hello girls, what a treat to see you together."

Bethany steps up like she's our spokesperson. "It's a girl's night. We're even spending the night at Hayley's house tonight. Her parents are going to let us use the hot tub."

Mrs. Cheri grins. "That sounds like a great evening. We won't keep you, it's our date night before Thanksgiving chaos begins. I think Sabrina counted seven side dishes we're making."

Wow. As long as my dad makes the mashed potatoes, I'm not looking for much else.

Jade's shock comes through her higher-than-usual pitched voice. "That's a lot of food. I hope you guys have a great Thanksgiving."

Pastor glances at Mrs. Cheri, who starts her hugs with Jade. "We will. Love you girls."

Once they continue their date, Bethany points to her favorite store that carries ripped jeans. For most sizes, but not mine. "Let's go in there. My parents gave me money."

It feels like a baseball is lodged in my throat. I bite my lip, praying words will come so I don't have to feel awkward like I did when we were school shopping.

Jade tugs at my arm. "Hayley, I'm not really into clothes shopping tonight. I have enough cash to look at makeup at the dollar store. Wanna go?"

I shoot Jade a sideways glance and catch her wink. She knows. And cares.

Jazmin seems to understand, too. "Jade, would you like us all to go? We can shop for clothes any time, right, Bethy?"

Bethany appears confused, but Jazmin elbows her and Bethany nods. "Right, right. This is a girl's night. Let's do stuff together."

We saunter down the mall to the dollar store and take over the makeup area. I find a lipstick that's pretty adult looking, but I remember Jade saying a while back it was what the older girls wore and the boys loved it.

"What do you think of this shade?" I hold it up and read the label. "Fire engine red."

Jade doesn't even look, but her answer is swift. "You don't need that Hayley, you're beautiful with a natural look."

The lipstick feels like I'm holding hot coals. I throw it back in the bin and let out a contented sigh as I glance at my group of friends.

It's going to be a great night.

CHAPTER TWENTY
SABRINA

I'm trying on my third sweater in near tears. *Girl, calm yourself. Your father is coming to Thanksgiving dinner. It isn't the queen.* I look at the black top and brown leggings in the mirror and sigh. The outfit is comfortable. It doesn't matter what my father thinks. I recall what my parents spoke over me after we prayed about inviting my father for the holiday.

Mom repeated it more than once that night. "You are altogether beautiful, my darling, beautiful in every way. It's true, because it's God's word. Song of Solomon, chapter four, verse seven. It's His proclamation over you, Sabrina."

Snapping back to the present, the doorbell rings. I check my watch and freeze. It's my father.

I procrastinate by putting my hair in a high ponytail and take my time walking down the stairs. Dad opens the door and gives his younger brother a hug. My father has a faded pair of black jeans and a cream sweater that looks like it has a coffee stain on the bottom.

"Chet, thanks for letting me come. I know it would have been easier to tell me to walk in traffic."

Dad slaps him on the shoulder as they part. "Nonsense. We prayed about it as a family. It was a joint decision."

The man I know more for drunken escapades than parenting lifts his head. "Really?"

I open my mouth and hope the words come out. "It's true. Happy Thanksgiving, Father."

He offers his open arms, and I walk awkwardly into them. As I give a quick hug, I realize his hands are shaking. He pulls away. "Sabrina, you look great. I can't wait to hear how you're doing. Chet said you're teaching."

That simple hug and response broke away enough of our pain that our conversation flowed from foyer to dinner table, and to the kitchen as we washed dishes.

"You helped Cheri with the turkey? It was one of the best meals I've ever had."

I hand him a plate to dry off. "Thanks. She's teaching me their traditions so when I move on my own, I'll know what to do."

He wipes at the same spot. "You've had it good, living here. You needed that. Sabrina, I'm really happy your life is coming together, in spite of me."

I dig in the soapy water, trying to avoid any knives. "Are you really done drinking?"

My father nearly drops the plate. "I want to say that I am, but I think that would be unwise. No alcoholic is ever recovered. I'm learning I have to take everything a day at a time. Sometimes, a second at a time. But I have forty-four days of sobriety. Nothing to sneeze at, not for me."

Now it's my turn to nearly drop the platter. "Wow. That's fantastic. Is there anything we can do to help?"

He smiles, and a beautiful speck of blue pops in his usually bloodshot eyes. "You already are."

I hand him another dish. "How's that?"

"You've been praying for me, and you let me join you today."

Once the dishes are done, we join my parents in the living room for some football. Before I can see what the score is, the doorbell rings. I rise first, still feeling full of mashed potatoes. "I'll get it."

I look through the peep hole and smile, opening the door. "Charlie. Happy Thanksgiving."

He has a fall arrangement of flowers in hand. "Hey, Sabrina. Happy Thanksgiving to you. You probably ate, but if you need a centerpiece, I have these for you." He thrusts them into my hand so fast that some of the stems bend.

I gesture him to come in and notice mom gawking, wide smile pasted on her face. "Thank you, that's so sweet. We did eat, but I can enjoy them because the table is clean. Can you stay for a while?"

Charlie stands still, hands jammed in his pockets. "Yes, but I wondered, would you be interested in taking a walk? With me?"

My eyes widen and it feels like someone turned the furnace on to volcanic temperatures. "Sure. Let me get my coat."

I stroll over to the closet and reach for it, my heart beating like a rock drummer on a solo. While I zip up, I trek over to my family. "Charlie and I are going to take a walk. I'll be back soon."

Dad winks. "No problem. Sweat some turkey off for me."

Mom almost sounds like she's going to sing her goodbye. "Have fun, you two!"

Charlie closes the door and bounds down the steps to the sidewalk. We dawdle quietly as we leave the driveway and start trekking the development.

"Did you eat dinner yet?"

He nods. "I ate way too much."

I roll my eyes. "Me too. This was a great idea. Maybe I won't gain a hundred pounds like usual."

Charlie stops. "Sabrina Wayson, stop talking like that."

It takes me a few steps to turn back and re-join him. "What do you mean?"

"You saying negative stuff about yourself. Do you know how beautiful you are?"

His words suspend time and melt my fears. "That's the nicest thing anyone has said to me."

He sighs. "I've wanted to say it to you for a long time. It's true. Your eyes are just, everything about you is so kind and inviting. And fun. You are the easiest to talk to. You're so giving, all the stuff you do at church and for girls, it's amazing." He reaches for my hand and holds it. "Sabrina, you're amazing."

It's tempting to stub my toe on purpose to make sure this is real. We re-start our stroll, and he doesn't drop my hand. "Well, how about you? You're handsome with that gorgeous hair of yours..." I pause to see if I've said too much, too fast. He grins, but we keep our pace, so I continue. "You're so smart. You'll have that PhD in no time. You've always encouraged me, and you're great making everyone around you feel important."

He tightens the grip on my hand. "It appears that we are big fans of each other."

My laughter echoes throughout the street. "I suppose we are. What do you suggest we do?"

Charlie stops and faces me. "Would you be interested in going on a date with me?"

I nod, wanting to race down the street and tell everyone this is the best Thanksgiving ever. As we cross streets and circle back, we've discussed possible date ideas, times, and what we like and don't. When we walk up my driveway, we've finalized plans to go to a dinner and a movie Saturday night.

"What should I wear?"

He chuckles. "It doesn't matter. Just remember I want to get to know you better, the beautiful Sabrina Wayson. I'm not interested in your outfits."

We hug before he announces his parents are expecting him, and he jogs across the street to his house. I wait before going back inside, holding my hands to my heart.

"Thank You, Father, for providing so much for me to be thankful for. My father, my parents, a job I love, ministry and girls I'm crazy about, and for Charlie." I look at my reflection in the living room window, seeing myself as I also spot my family still watching the game. My hair's windblown, I feel bloated from all the food.

But the words are becoming real to me. I'm beautiful.

IF YOU LOVED YOU'RE BEAUTIFUL:

It would mean a lot if you would leave a review on Amazon and Goodreads. The more reviews a book has, the more publicity it receives on Amazon.

A review can be as short as "I really liked it!" If you aren't sure what to write, you can share a couple things that stood out to you, as long as you don't give the plot away. If you know us "in real life," don't mention that. Thank you for taking the time to share your thoughts and to help us get this important message out to girls of all ages.

THANK YOU!

If you have ever been told anything close to what Hayley and Sabrina heard, please know that it is not the truth. The true defeated one, the devil, has limited resources and will use whatever bag of tricks he can that will work. He loves to lie and make us feel like we are defeated, because the truth is, he's defeated. We were created as God's masterpiece, the piece de resistance. We are beautiful. YOU are beautiful. That is the truth. Receive and live it out, and please let others know about this book. We truly want to change lives with our words, and one of the most important messages a girl can hear is she's beautiful!

Surrendering Stinkin' Thinkin'

Book One
Surrendering Stinkin' Thinkin'
for Girls 10-100

You're Beautiful

Hannah Arduini & Julie Arduini

You're Beautiful---Hayley Atkinson withdraws from her friends and new opportunities with the new mentoring group, Linked, after she is told a lie that she believes is true about herself. Sabrina Wayson is a mentor in Linked who feels she can't encourage girls because she's struggling as much as they are. Can they surrender the lies and find freedom?

Coming Soon:

You're Amazing---Jazmin has always been a natural with dance, and now that she's in junior high, she's been promoted to an advanced group with older girls. For the first time, her favorite activity isn't easy, and she feels left out. Lena enjoyed going out with friends, but after getting married and having young children, she doesn't get invited out much anymore, and she finds motherhood exhausting. Can these two members of Linked let go of their frustration and realize how cherished they are?

You're Brilliant---Bethany has a lot of changes in her life as a new teenager, but she decides to tackle it with her offbeat humor. No one laughs with her, and even worse, her classmates abandon her, making Bethany feel rejected. Mrs. Cheri is a pastor's wife who loves her life, but new commitments have her overwhelmed. A joke aimed at her goes straight to her heart, and she's convinced she's not good at anything she's been asked to do. Can these two stop believing lies about themselves and embrace the changes in their lives?

Coming Soon:

Anchored, Book 1 in the Surrendering Opinions Series. Contemporary Romance.

"The Collins Six" made history with their unique birth story, and stayed in the national spotlight with their tragedy.

Now that they are young adults, each sibling tries to find their own identity and romance that matches the love their parents had. Can they surrender the plans and thoughts everyone who helped raise them has and find freedom?

Anchored

Coming Soon:

Anchored, Book 1 in the Surrendering Opinions Series. Contemporary Romance.

"The Collins Six" made history with their unique birth story, and stayed in the national spotlight with their tragedy.

Now that they are young adults, each sibling tries to find their own identity and romance that matches the love their parents had. Can they surrender the plans and thoughts everyone who helped raise them has and find freedom?

Anchored

Anchored Prologue
1992

Julia Turmeric stared at the cordless phone in her hand. The buzz of the newsroom swarmed around her, but her focus remained on the disconnected call.

A set of finger snaps brought her back to reality. "Jules! What's going on? I've been talking to you about Hussein's latest statement and I didn't even get an eye roll."

She turned her head to her cameraman and held up the phone. "It's my best friend from back home, Lisa Collins."

Her colleague nodded. "Oh, right. The morning anchor at that little station Upstate, right?"

Julia bit her lip as she replaced the phone to the base. "Yeah. She's pregnant."

"I remember you saying something about it, that her and the husband had been trying for a while. She okay?"

Her expression still vacant, she sighed. "They just learned they are carrying sextuplets. I knew they were doing infertility treatments and there was a chance of multiples, but this?" She ran a finger through her long, ebony, straight hair. "The doctors asked them to reduce, she had some term for it, but she's real serious about her faith. Very pro-life."

He picked up a tripod. "She's keeping all of them?"

She tapped the camera. "And Lisa wants us to document their story."

December, 1992

Julia unbuckled the seatbelt and stared at the ranch-style home in front of her. "How are Lisa and Paul taking care of six babies in this little house?"

Her cameraman took the keys out of the ignition and shrugged. "This is your old Big Flats neighborhood, right? You grew up with brothers and sisters."

She pulled down the visor mirror and applied fresh lipstick. "Not six born at once." She snapped the visor back in place and blotted her mouth with a tissue. "If anyone can do this, it's Lisa. That girl could make the hardest person smile and tell their story to her for the camera. I still don't understand how she didn't keep our pact. In college we said we'd go national together."

"Love will do it all the time." He chuckled. "Ask my ex-wives."

Julia rolled her eyes and gestured toward the house. "Can you get some exterior shots? I'm going in."

She closed her eyes for a moment, and took a deep breath before ringing the doorbell. Julia recognized Lisa's mom, Gail Bell, when she opened the door, cradling a baby.

The instant grandmother of six wore a wide smile. "If it isn't little JT from down the street. Come in."

Julia remembered the childhood name for Lisa's mom. "Hi, Mama G. Who do you have here?"

Gail's shaky laugh echoed in the foyer. "If he didn't have a tag, I wouldn't know. This is James Matthew Collins, number four of six."

Six babies seemed so surreal. Julia looked down the hall and could see a swing in motion.

"My cameraman will be inside soon. We have a lot to do. Can I see Paul and Lisa?"

Mama G. nodded and strolled down the hall to what Julia guessed was a living room. The couch and TV were there, but everything else was baby related. Swings. Baby chairs. Cradles.

Julia could barely take it all in. Two people were in front of her on the couch, each holding a baby. On the floor a woman sat near the swings, watching the remaining three fight sleep as they rocked back and forth.

Gail lowered her voice. "Lisa, Paul. Julian's here."

The two rose from the couch and faced Julia. Lisa navigated through the maze of equipment to reach her friend. "Julia! Thank you so much for doing this. It means everything to Paul and me that you're the one covering our journey."

Julia leaned in for a quick hug. "Are you kidding? Do you know how many stations around the world want to interview the parents of the multiples who not only refused selective reduction, but had them stay the longest in the womb? You all are medical miracles."

Lisa glanced at Paul, who was at her side. "It's all God. He blessed and took care of us."

Paul chuckled. "And we pray He keeps providing. We need all the help we can get."

July 1995

Julia touched the ends of her newly-cut hair. The humidity in New York City seemed extra miserable, but the five-hour trek to Corning didn't seem to provide any relief. The short hair took getting used to, but she was glad she did it.

Walt shook his head as the Collins home came into view. "Look at all the tricycles."

"It's crazy. At least that means the kids are more mobile than the first time we met them. I can't believe the community pitched in and had this home built for them."

He nodded and pulled into the long, blacktop driveway. Three of the kids were in the yard blowing bubbles. "Viewers eat this up. They love this family. Lisa was smart to lock you in as a lifetime interviewer no matter what job you have, or what station."

Julie smiled. Lisa may have left the news business for home life with the kids, but she was savvy. Every year the media sent Paul and Lisa publicity requests to see the kids and interview them. Lisa found a lawyer willing to draft an exclusive agreement that gave Julia the only access to what reporters called the kids, "The Collins Six."

"And now that I'm co-anchor if Rise and Shine, I think ratings will skyrocket. Moms watch the show, and they adore Lisa." Julia reached for her briefcase and looked out the window. "Speaking of, here she is."

Lisa sauntered over to the news van, her long hair piled on top of her head. "Julia. Walt. It can't be another year already."

The two exited the vehicle and greeted the Faces and Places magazine's Mom of the Year with a hug. "What's three years old like? Does it get worse than terrible two?" Walt opened the back of the van. Lisa shook her head. "All I can say is if your producer wants a transparent look at 'The Collins Six,' you're going to have plenty of footage."

Julia heard a screech, followed by a cry. One of the boys held an empty bubble bottle while one of the girls had wet, soapy hair. Julia tapped her favorite cameraman. "You can start by taping that."

September 1997

Julia tripped over a backpack on her way to the spacious Collins kitchen. Jimmy and Kelly, babies four and five, were eating at the kitchen table. "Hey, guys. Can I ask you a couple questions?"

Jimmy looked to his sister, then to Julia. "Is it for TV?"

She nodded.

He narrowed his eyes and took another bite. "Are you gonna ask about school?"

Julia smiled. "Yes, that's what everyone wants to know about."

He put the bread on the plate. "I can make it easy. We all hate it."

Julia bit her lip to kill the temptation to laugh. She glanced at Kelly, who nodded. "Hate it."

January 2001

Julia placed a piece of hair behind her ear as she looked at her notes for her upcoming interview with the latest A-lister actress. The morning show and evening magazine duties gave her a lot of assignments with Hollywood's elite, but few gave Julia joy in prepping for the meeting.

She took a sip of her coffee and heard a knock on the door. Glancing at her office clock, it was late in the evening for visitors. "Who is it?"

His voice cracked. "Walt."

Julia stood and jogged to the door. He was always home and with his family once his assignments were done. She opened it, ready to invite him in, when she saw his hands shake and his eyes full of tears. "What's wrong?"

"I told the brass I would be the one to tell you."

Her eyebrows furrowed as she tried to discern what he was saying.

"Julia, there's been a terrible accident back in your hometown."

She felt the pit form and enlarge, as she instantly thought of her parents and siblings. "Dad? Mom?"

Walt shook his head. "Lisa and a couple of the kids."

Julia felt her knees sliding beneath her. "Tell me they are okay."

She never, in all her years choosing Walt as her cameraman, saw him cry.

"Lisa's gone."

Anchored

Acknowledgements:

Hannah: Mrs. Gordon, Ms. Yargo, Mrs. Vrabel, and Ms. Lori, thank you for encouraging me and believing in me. For asking about this book and how I am doing.

Everyone at Generations, past and present, especially Olivia, Angelina and Mrs. Summer, for spending time with me at Starbucks and getting mani/pedis. For Mr. Duane and Mrs. Tracie and everyone involved in respite nights and Night to Shine for making me feel extra beautiful.

Pastor Matt, Erica, Miss Deb, Miss Heidi, Miss Shannon, I appreciate you having my back at youth group.

Amilia, Kayla, Kaylee, Aalayah, Tatyanna, Maleah, Mercedes, Honesti, and Bella, your friendship and encouragement mean so much to me. I love you guys.

For Mrs. Rhonda, for helping us come up with the name of the series just by being Southern.

Cole, Heidi, and your fun families. Thank you for running for me! #coleRuns4Hannah

Randy, Mandy, Oliver, Matt, Stephanie, and James, I love my Wisconsin family.

Grandma, Aunt Crista, and Landon. You always cheer me on. Thank you! Brian, you're a great brother, even if I pretend to be annoyed by you.

Dad, thanks for everything you do for our family and how you make me smile. And for lunch money.

Mom, thanks for taking me out of my comfort zone by hearing my story idea and making it real. For believing in me.

Jesus, You told my parents before I was born that I would be an overcomer. Thank You for being a Keeper of Promises.

Julie: Hannah, you challenge and inspire me daily to keep shining bright for Christ even when times are tough. In a difficult season, you chose better over bitter. More than that, you came up with a series that I believe was God sent to encourage many. You are amazing.

Scribes 202, this book wasn't a normal submission given my contemporary romance background, but you dove in without reservation or hesitation. Thank you for all your help. I couldn't write without you.

Shirley, Ruth, Kara, Deb, Tracie, Summer, Brenda, Rita, Noreen, and Amy. Your prayers literally cover everything in my life. Thank you for keeping this project and our family in prayer.

To the Engaged Book Club, thanks for your enthusiasm and support. When I first mentioned this series, you were among the first to cheer Hannah and me along.

To the real "Linked" ministry, the story and conflict are fiction, but the love, prayers, and friendships between the ages were definitely borne out of everything we experienced in this real ministry. Looking forward to much more "Generations" to come. Pastor Matt, Erica, Shannon, Deb, and Heidi, I never thought God would place me in youth ministry to serve. I'm so glad He did.

Pastor Gary and Rhonda Gray for allowing me to share sermon notes, and for Rhonda inspiring the name of the series and being all around wonderful.

Cheryl, Holly B., Holly H., Amy, Dar, and Julie, thank you for being treasured friends I look forward to visiting. I wish it was more often.

Randy, Mandy, Oliver, Matt, Stephanie, and James, thank you for loving Hannah, Brian, and me from the first moment we entered your lives.

Brian, you had your own refiner's fire at the same time Hannah was trusting God through hers. The pure gold that is showing itself from that season blesses and teaches me. Keep believing Him, even and especially when the world disappoints.

Tom, thanks for being among the first to show me true freedom comes when I surrender negative thinking. I've grown because you taught me to give people the benefit of the doubt, and reminded me that God promised to lead us through the fire, not around it. Thanks for asking.

Jesus, I didn't see any of this coming, the adversity or the story. You did, and I appreciate the grace as I processed the hurt, grief, lament, and the beginning of healing. Not a word, not a breath is possible without You. It is all for the furthering of Your Kingdom and Your glory.

Other Julie Arduini Titles
Surrendering Time Series
(Contemporary Romance)

Entrusted:

A city-girl produces a lot of change for a mountain grocer. A romance about surrendering loss, change, and wanting to belong. This is a free eBook on juliearduini.com.

Entangled:

A single mom has been given everything to make her dreams come true, but regret keeps her from enjoying her blessings. Can her reliable, truck-driving boyfriend help her surrender her past?

Engaged:

A career woman returns to her rural hometown after her dreams crumble and she has no other plans. Can the local paramedic come to her rescue?

Finding Freedom Through Surrender: A 30-Day Devotional:

Features the characters and themes from
Entrusted, Entangled, and Engaged. Perfect
whether you've enjoyed or are new to the series

Multi-Author Devotional Workbook about Infertility

A Walk in the Valley: Six authors share their own infertility stories from diagnosis to where they are now. Includes questions for reflection.

The Julie Arduini Newsletter

Subscribe and receive free eBook of Entrusted, Book 1 in the Surrendering Time Series. Monthly email with writing updates, recipes, giveaways, contests, book recommendations and more. Visit juliearduini.com to subscribe for free.

Follow Julie Arduini and other
Inspy Romance authors:
Blog:
http://inspyromance.com
Twitter:
http://twitter.com/inspyromance
Facebook:
http://facebook.com/inspyromance
Pinterest:
http://pinterest.com/inspyromance

CHRISTIANS READ

Follow Julie Arduini and other Christian authors at Christians Read.

Blog:

http://christiansread.wordpress.com

Facebook:

http://facebook.com/christiansread

Twitter:

http://twitter.com/christiansread

Looking for
an Encouraging Speaker?

Julie Arduini is passionate about encouraging audiences to find freedom through surrender. She's able to speak on a wide range of surrender topics, the writing process, family, motherhood, and her own books.

Learn more by contacting her at juliearduini@juliearduini.com.

Regan's Acts of Kindness

Although I never met Regan, her parents spent a lot of time with our family when we lived in Upstate NY. Regan was taken from them in January 2017. She would have turned four in March.
Everyone who loved Regan wants her to be remembered.
Here are different ways you can help make that happen:

- **Like Regan's Acts of Kindness on Facebook and participate.**
http://facebook.com/RegansActsofKindness

- **Paint Rocks and Hide them in appropriate places in your community.** Check the Facebook page above to learn how to tag them to keep the kindness flowing.

- **Visit Regan's Corner at The Wild Animal Park in Chittenango, New York**
http://thewildpark.com

About the Authors:

Hannah Arduini is in the eighth grade and lives outside of Youngstown, Ohio. She loves fashion, Starbucks, and serving at church. She has a brother who lives at home, and siblings that live in Wisconsin. She also has two nephews. *You're Beautiful* is her first published book.

Julie Arduini loves to encourage readers to surrender the good, the bad, and ---maybe one day---the chocolate. She's the author of the contemporary romance series Surrendering Time, featuring ENTRUSTED, ENTANGLED, and ENGAGED. FINDING FREEDOM THROUGH SURRENDER is her 30-day devotional using the surrender themes and characters from the series. She shares her infertility story in A WALK IN THE VALLEY. She blogs every other Wednesday for Christians Read, and also is a blogger for Inspy Romance. She resides in Ohio with her husband and two children. Learn more by visiting her at http://juliearduini.com.

Made in the USA
Columbia, SC
15 February 2018